Confession of a Murderer

Joseph Roth titles
published by The Overlook Press

The Radetzky March

The Emperor's Tomb

Tarabas

Confession of a Murderer

Job

Flight Without End

Hotel Savoy

Right and Left and *The Legend of the Holy Drinker*

The Silent Prophet

The Spider's Web and *Zipper and His Father*

CONFESSION
OF A MURDERER
Told in One Night

Joseph Roth

Translated from the German by
Desmond I. Vesey

THE OVERLOOK PRESS
Woodstock & New York

This paperback edition first published in the United States in 2003 by
The Overlook Press, Peter Mayer Publishers, Inc.
Woodstock & New York

WOODSTOCK:
One Overlook Drive
Woodstock, NY 12498
www.overlookpress.com
[for individual orders, bulk and special sales, contact our Woodstock office]

NEW YORK:
141 Wooster Street
New York, NY 10012

Library of Congress Cataloging-in-Publication Data

Roth, Joseph, 1894–1939.
Confession of a murderer.
I. Title.
PT2635.084C6   1985   833'.912   84-20580

Book design and type formatting by Bernad Schleifer
Manufactured in the United States of America
ISBN 1-58567-384-6
1 3 5 7 9 8 6 4 2

Confession of a Murderer

SOME YEARS AGO I was living in the Rue des Quatres Vents. My window looked across the street at a Russian restaurant called the "Tari-Bari." I often used to eat there. At any hour of the day one could get *borscht,* grilled fish, and boiled beef. I sometimes got up late in the day. The French restaurants, in which the customary hours for lunching were strictly adhered to, were already preparing for their evening meals. But in the Russian restaurant time played no part. A tin clock hung on the wall. Sometimes it had stopped, sometimes it was wrong; its purpose seemed to be not to tell the time, but to ridicule it. No one looked at the clock. Most of the guests in this restaurant were Russian emigrants. And even those amongst them who, in their own country, might have had a sense of punctuality and exactitude, seemed now, in a foreign land, either to have lost it or to be ashamed of displaying it. Yes, it was as though those emigrants were consciously demonstrating against the calculating, the all calculating and so very calculated, deliberations of the European West; as though they were at pains not only to remain real Russians, but also to *play* at being "real Russians," to live up to the European conception of what Russians should be. So the inaccurate or inactive clock in the restaurant "Tari–Bari" was more than a necessary requisite; it was a symbol. The laws of time seemed to have been rescinded. And sometimes I noticed that even the Russian taxi drivers, who most certainly had to keep definite working hours, were as little concerned with the passage of time as the other emigrants who had no profession and who lived on the charity of their wealthier compatriots. Of such unemployed Russians there were many in the Restaurant "Tari–Bari." They sat there at all times of the day and evening, and even late into the night when the host began to reckon up with the waiters and the outer door was already bolted and only a single lamp remained burning over the self-locking safe. Not till the waiters and the proprietor went did the guests leave the dining room. Some among them, who lacked a shelter or were drunk, were allowed by the host to pass the night in the restaurant. It was too much trouble to wake them—and even if they had been awoken, they would have had to have sought sanctuary with some other of their countrymen.

Although, as I have said, I mostly got up very late in the day, sometimes when I happened to wander across to my window in the morning, I could see that the "Tari–Bari" was doing brisk business. People were going in and out. They apparently took an early breakfast there, and sometimes even an alcoholic breakfast. For I saw several come stumbling out who had entered with perfectly steady feet. Individual faces and figures became familiar to me. And amongst those who were unusual enough to take my attention was a man who, I was led to assume, was to be found in the restaurant "Tari-Bari" at any time of the day. For whenever I walked to my window in the morning, I could see him across the way, standing in front of the door of the restaurant, in the company of customers or greeting customers. And whenever I came in to lunch late in the afternoon, I saw him sitting at some table or other, talking with the guests. And when I came into the "Tari-Bari" late in the evening—before "closing time" as business people say—to drink a last schnapps, the stranger would be sitting by the bar, helping the host and the waiters with their reckoning-up. In the course of time he seemed to become accustomed to the sight of me and to regard me as a sort of colleague. He conceded to me the distinction of being an habitué like himself—and after a few weeks he greeted me with the understanding and expressive smile which old acquaintances reserve for one another. I must admit that at first this smile disturbed me—for whenever he smiled, his otherwise honest and kindly face took on a not exactly repulsive, but somehow suspicious expression. His smile was not a bright one, it did not light up his face, for in spite of all his friendliness it was dark, it swept like a shadow over his countenance, a friendly shadow. And so it would have been preferable to me if the man had not smiled.

Of course I smiled back out of politeness. And I hoped that those reciprocal smiles would remain for the time being, or even for a longer period, the sole expression of our acquaintanceship. Yes, within myself I even decided to avoid the place, should the stranger one day address himself to me. But in time this thought, too, passed from my mind. I accustomed myself to the shadowy smile, I began to take an interest in this man. And soon I felt a desire to become more closely acquainted with him.

It is now time for me to describe him in somewhat more detail. He was a large man, broad shouldered, with fair hair turning gray. His eyes were clear, sometimes flashing, never clouded with alcohol; and he always looked the person he was addressing straight in the face. An enormous, carefully kept, horizontal mustache divided the upper part of his broad face from the lower; and both parts of his face were equally large. Because of this, his appearance struck one as somehow weary and meaningless, as though it hid no secret. I myself have seen hundreds of such men in Russia, dozens of such men in Germany and other countries. Particularly striking in this huge man were his long sensitive hands, and his soft, quiet, almost inaudible step; in fact, all his movements were slow, shy, and cautious. For that reason it seemed to me sometimes that his face nevertheless hid a secret, as though his open, lucid straightforwardness were only a pretense; it seemed that the man only gazed so steadily with his blue eyes at the people with whom he spoke, because he was thinking that people might have a reason for mistrusting him if he did not do so. And yet in the face of that glance, I had to keep saying to myself that if he could give such a complete although naïve representation of straightforwardness personified, he must in actual fact possess a large degree of straightforwardness. The smile with which he greeted me was perhaps only dank from embarrassment; although, during the smile, his great teeth gleamed and his mustache took on a golden shimmer as though momentarily it lost its grayness and became even fairer than before. You can see that I became more and more attracted towards this man. And soon I even began, when I reached the door of the restaurant, to look forward to seeing him, as much as I looked forward to the familiar schnapps and the familiar greeting of our fat host.

I had never let it be known in the "Tari-Bari" that I understood Russian. But once, when I was sitting at a table with two chauffeurs, they asked me, straight out, what nationality I was. I answered that I was a German, but if they intended discussing any secrets in front of me, no matter what the language, they had better do so after I had left, if they didn't mind. For I understood most European languages. But just at that moment another table became free, so I got up and left the chauffeurs alone with their secrets. Also they could not ask me, as was obviously their intention, whether I understood Russian. And so still no one knew that.

But they discovered it one day, or rather one evening; or, to be quite precise, late one night. And that was thanks to the man with the graying hair, who at that time was sitting exactly opposite the bar, exceptionally silent and gloomy, if that description could ever be really applied to him.

I came in shortly before midnight, with the intention of drinking a last schnapps and then leaving immediately. So at first I did not look for a table, but remained standing at the bar between two other late customers, who also seemed to have come in for only one schnapps, but who, contrary to their original plan, must have been there for some considerable time; for several empty and half-empty glasses were standing before them, while they possibly thought that they had still drunk only one. Time often passes quickly like that, when one stands at the bar instead of sitting at a table. When one sits at a table, one sees every second how much one has drunk, and the number of empty glasses marks the movement of the clock. But should one just "step in," as they say, to a restaurant, and remain standing at the bar, one drinks and drinks and firmly believes that it all belongs to the single "step" orig-inally intended. I myself noticed this on that particular evening. For, like the other two, I also drank one and then another and then a third, and I still stood there like one of those every hurrying, ever dilatory people who come into a house, refuse to take off their coats, keep hold of the door handle, intending every moment to say good-bye, and who yet stay longer than if they had at the beginning come right in and sat down. The other two customers were talking quietly with the host in Russian. The gray-haired man could certainly only half hear what was being said at the bar. He was sitting some distance away from us. I could see him in the mirror behind the bar, and he seemed in no way inclined to listen to the conversation or even to take part in it. I, too, as usual pretended to understand nothing. But suddenly a sentence caught my ear. I could not help hearing it. The sentence ran: "Why is our murderer so gloomy today?" One of the two customers had said this and at the same moment he pointed with his finger at the reflection in the mirror behind the bar. Involuntarily I turned towards the gray-haired man and thereby revealed that I had understood the question. The others immediately stared at me somewhat mistrustfully, but their expressions were mainly of astonishment. The Russians have, not without justification, a terror of police spies, and at all costs I wanted to avoid them suspecting me of being one. But at the same time the unusual description, "our murderer," intrigued me so much that I immediately determined to ask why the gray-haired man was so called. When I turned round I noticed that the man had also heard this question. He nodded, smiling. And he would probably have answered for himself, had I remained indifferent and had I not in that short minute become an object of doubt and mistrust. "So you are a Russian?" the host asked me. "No," I was about to reply, but to my amazement the gray-haired man answered behind my back: "Our friend here understands Russian, but he is a German. It was only his discretion that kept him quiet." "That's so," I agreed, and I turned round and said: "Thank you, sir!" "Not at all," he said, and stood up and came towards me. "My name is Golubchik," he said, "Semjon Semjonovitch Golubchik." We shook hands. The host and the other two customers laughed. "How is it that you know so much about me?" I asked. "One has not been a member of the Russian secret police for nothing," answered Golubchik. I immediately envisaged a fantastic story. This man here, I thought, was an old official in the Ochrana and had killed a Communist spy in Paris; and that was why these White Russian emigrants so harmlessly and almost affectionately named him "our murderer," and had no aversion to him. Yes, perhaps they were all four involved.

"And how is it that you know our language?" asked one of the customers. And again Golubchik answered: "He was on the Eastern front during the war and served in the so-called 'Army of Occupation.'" "True enough," I said. "And later," continued Golubchik, "he was again in Russia; that is to say, not in Russia but in the Union of Soviet Socialist Republics. He was working for an important newspaper. He is a writer." I was amazed at this precise information about myself. For I had drunk a fair amount, and in this condition I can hardly distinguish the miraculous from the matter-of-course. I was very polite and said a little pompously: "I thank you for the interest which you have for so long taken in me, and for the distinction which you have thereby conferred on me." They all laughed. And the host said: "He talks like an old Petersburg alderman!" With that, all doubts as to my standing were allayed. Yes, they even regarded me benevolently, and there followed four more rounds in which we all drank to each other's health.

The host went to the door, locked it, put out a number of the lights, and invited us all to sit down. The hands of the clock pointed at half-past eight. I had no watch on me, and for one of the guests to enquire about the time seemed to me unseemly. I thought rather that I should be spending half the night there, or possibly the whole night. A large carafe of schnapps stood before us. In my estimation it would, at least, have to be half emptied. So I asked: "Why did they speak in such an extraordinary way of you just now, Herr Golubchik?"

"That is my nickname," he answered, "but again, it is not only a nickname. Many years ago I killed a man and—as I then believed—a woman also."

"A political assassination?" asked our host, and thus it became clear to me that the others also knew nothing, except for the nickname.

"Nothing like it!" said Semjon. "I am in no way a political personality. I am not interested in public affairs. I prefer private ones. Those are the only things that interest me. I am a good Russian—even if a Russian from a frontier land. I was born in Wolhynia. But I have never been able to understand the companions of my youth, with their desperate desire to dedicate their lives to some mad or, for all I care, sensible idea. No! Believe me, a man's private life, simple humanity, is more important, greater, more tragic than all the public affairs in the world. And perhaps to modern ears that sounds absurd. But I believe that, and I will believe it to my last hour. I could never have aroused in myself enough political passion to kill a man for political reasons. Neither do I believe that political criminals are better or finer than others; provided, of course, that one is not of the opinion that a criminal, of whatever sort, can never be a fine person. Take myself for example. I have killed and yet I consider myself to be a good man. A foul creature, or to speak more plainly, a woman, drove me to murder."

"Very interesting," said our host.

"Not at all. Very ordinary," said Semjon Semjonovitch modestly. "And yet not quite so ordinary. I can tell you my story quite shortly. And you will see that it is only a simple tale."

He began. And the story was neither short nor commonplace. Therefore I have decided to write it down here.

"I HAVE PROMISED TO tell you a short story, but I see now that I must go far back for the real beginning of it all, and so I beg you not to become impatient with me. I said earlier that private affairs are the only things that interest me. I must return to that point. By that statement I mean that, if one examines life closely enough, one must of necessity come to the conclusion that all the so-called great historical events in this world can, in fact, be traced back to some moment in the private life of their author, or to several such moments. Not for nothing—that is, not without some private impulse—can one become a Field Marshal or a Socialist or a reactionary; and all great and noble and despicable deeds, which have to some extent altered the history of this world, are the results of some quite unimportant occurrence of which we have no knowledge. I told you earlier that I was once a police spy. (After this, I shall simply call myself a spy, but you must remember that that is never meant in the international sense. I was simply a hireling employed to spy upon my own people.) Well, I have often racked my brains to discover why I, of all people, should have been chosen to follow such an accursed profession—for there is no grace in it, and it is certainly not pleasing to God. Today it is still the same; without a doubt, I am possessed by a devil. Of course you know that I no longer make my living by spying, but I can never give it up—I can never give it up. There must be a special demon of espionage. If someone should interest me especially, as for example this gentleman here, the writer"—Golubchik nodded towards me—"I could have no peace, or rather it would leave me no peace, until I had found out who he was, where he lived, and where he came from. For, of course, I know considerably more than you imagine. You live across the road, and some mornings you look out of the window while you are dressing. But you are not the subject of this story, I am. So I'll get on. My profession was not pleasing to God, but His inscrutable will had selected it for me.

Well, you know my name, gentlemen—my friends, I would rather say. For it *is* better to say "my friends" when one tells a story, in the good old-fashioned way. My name is, as you know, Golubchik.* I ask you whether that is fitting and just. I was always big and strong; even as a boy I far exceeded in size and bodily strength my companions, and yet I had to be called Golubchik. Well, there is some-

*Golubchik means, in Russian, "little dove."

thing more to it than that; for that was not my name by right—that is, by natural right. Golubchik was only the name of my legitimate father. Actually, my real name, my natural one, the name of my natural father, was—Krapotkin. And I note that even now I cannot speak that name without a certain evil pride. So you see, I was an illegitimate child. As you probably know, Prince Krapotkin owned estates in every part of Russia. And one day the desire came to him to purchase an estate in Wolhynia. Such people had, indeed, their whims. On this occasion he learned to know my father and my mother. My father was head forester. The prince had actually decided to dismiss all those employed by the former owner of the estate. But when he saw my mother, he dismissed all—except my father. And so it came about. My father, the forester Golubchik, was a simple man. Imagine to yourselves an ordinary fair-haired forester in the ordinary forester's dress, and you have a picture of my legitimate father. His father, my grandfather, had been a serf. And so you will understand that the forester Golubchik had nothing to say against Prince Krapotkin, his new master, paying frequent visits to my mother at an hour when most married women in our country are accustomed to be lying at the side of their own husbands. Well, I need say no more; nine months later I came into the world, and for the previous three months my real father had been living in St. Petersburg. He sent money. He was a prince, and he behaved himself exactly as a prince should. For the rest of her life my mother never forgot him. I infer that from the fact that, after me, she never brought another child into the world. Which implies that, after the affair with Krapotkin, she refused "to fulfill her marital duties," as the law books put it. I myself can remember that they never slept together in the same bed, the forester Golubchik and my mother. My mother slept in the kitchen, on an improvised couch made up on a broad wooden bench just below the icon; while my father slept alone in the large double bed in the next room. For he earned enough to be able to afford both a front room and a kitchen. We lived on the edge of the so-called "black forest"—for there was also a lighter birch forest, while ours was a pine one. We lived alone, about two or three versts away from the nearest village which was called Woroniaki. Taken all in all, my legitimate father, the forester Golubchik, was a kindly man. I never heard a quarrel between him and my mother. They both of them knew what stood between them, and they never spoke of it. But one day—I must have been about eight years old at the time—a peasant from Woroniaki came to the house and asked for the forester, who at that hour was out in the woods. This man remained sitting in the kitchen, although my mother told him that her husband would not be home until late that evening. "Well, I've time enough," he said. "I can wait till this evening, and till midnight, and even later. I can wait until I am locked up. And that won't be for another day at least." "Why should they lock you up?" asked my mother. "Because I have just strangled my daugh-

ter Arina with my own hands," answered the peasant smiling. I was crouching beside the stove; neither my mother
nor the peasant took the slightest notice of me, and I can
remember the scene in the minutest detail. I shall never
forget it! I shall never forget how the man smiled, and how
at those terrible words, he looked at his outstretched hands.
My mother, who was at that moment kneading dough, laid
down the water and the flour on the table, crossed herself,
then folded her hands over her blue apron, stepped up to
our visitor and asked: "You strangled your daughter?"
"Yes," answered the man." "But why, in God's name?"
"Because she gave herself to your husband, the forester
Semjon Golubchik. That is his name?" The peasant said all
this with a smile, with a concealed smile that peeped out
from behind his words like the moon from behind dark
clouds. "That is my fault," said my mother. I can still hear
that sentence, as though she had spoken it yesterday. I can
remember her very words. (Although at the time I did not
understand them.) She crossed herself again. Then she took
me by the hand. She left the peasant sitting in our kitchen
and went with me into the forest, continually calling the
name of Golubchik. Nobody answered. We returned to the
house and the man was still sitting there. "Would you like
some broth?" asked my mother as we sat down to eat.
"No," answered our guest, smiling politely, "but if you, perhaps, have some *samogonka* in the house—
I would not refuse it." My mother poured him out a glass
of our home-distilled spirits, which he drank; and I can

remember clearly how he threw back his head and how I could see by the rippling of his bristly neck that the schnapps was running down his throat. He drank and drank and still remained sitting there. At last the sun went down—it may have been a day in early autumn—and my father came back. "Ah, Pantalejmon!" he said. The peasant stood up and said quietly: "Come outside with me." "Why?" asked the forester. "A few hours ago," the man answered, still quite calmly, "I killed Arina."

My father immediately went out with him. They remained away a long time. It might well have been an hour. My mother was on her knees before the icon in the kitchen. There was not a sound to be heard. It was already night. The little red lamp under the icon was the only light in the room, and never until that hour had I been afraid of it. My mother was kneeling the whole time and praying, and still my father did not come. I was crouching beside the stove. At last, it might have been three or more hours later, I heard steps and several voices outside the house. They were bringing my father home. Four men were carrying him. The forester Golubchik must have been a considerable weight. He was bleeding all over. Probably the father of his mistress had done that to him.

Well, I will be brief. The forester never recovered from those blows. He could no longer pursue his occupation. A few weeks later he died, and they buried him on an icy winter's day. I can still remember vividly that the grave-diggers who came to fetch him wore thick woollen mittens and yet had to beat their bodies with both hands to keep warm. They loaded my father on to a sledge. My mother and I sat in another, and during the drive the glittering frost sprayed a hundred thousand beautiful crystal needles into my face. Actually, I was joyful. The burial of my father counts among the happier memories of my childhood.

Passons!—as the French say. It was not long before I went to school. And, alert as I was, I soon discovered that I was the son of Krapotkin. I noticed it in the attitude of the teachers; and once, in spring, on a memorable day, when Krapotkin himself came to visit his estate, I knew it for certain. The village of Woroniaki was decorated in honor of the occasion. They hung garlands at both ends of the village street. They even collected a band, composed entirely of wind instruments, and some singers as well. They practiced for a whole week before, under the guidance of the schoolmaster. But during that week my mother would not let me go to school, and I only learned about the preparations by roundabout means. And one day Krapotkin really came. Straight to us. He ignored the street with the garlands, he ignored the band, he ignored the singers, and he came straight to our house. He had a beautiful, dark, slightly silvery beard; he smelt of cigars, and his hands were very long, very thin, very dry, almost withered. He stroked my head, asked me questions, turned me around a few times, looked at my hands, my ears, my eyes, my hair. Then he said that my ears were dirty and so were my fingernails.

He took out an ivory penknife and in two minutes carved out of an ordinary piece of wood a little man with a beard and long arms. (Later I heard that he was a renowned wood-carver.) Then he spoke for a while quietly with my mother, and then he left us.

Since that day, my friends, I knew without a doubt that I was not the son of Golubchik, but of Krapotkin. Of course I was very sorry that the Prince had disdained to pass through the decorated village, and had missed the music and the songs. It would have been best, so it seemed to me, if he had driven through the village in a marvelous carriage, drawn by four snow-white horses, with me at his side. On such an occasion, I would have been recognized by all, by the teacher, by the peasants, by the servants, and even by the authorities, as the legitimate, almost heaven-sent, successor to the Prince. And the songs and the music and the garlands would have been for me rather than for my father. Yes, my friends, that is what I was like at that time: arrogant, vain, afflicted with boundless imagination and extremely egotistic. On that occasion I never gave the slightest thought to my mother. Although, indeed, I realized to a certain extent that it was a disgrace for a woman to have a child by any man other than her own husband. But neither my mother's disgrace nor my own was impor- tant. On the contrary, it pleased me, and I preened myself greatly, not only because from the day of my birth I was marked with a distinctive brand, but also because I was the natural son of our Prince. But now, after everything had become as clear as day, the name of Golubchik annoyed me more and more, especially because everyone spoke it so scornfully after the death of the forester and since the Prince had visited my mother. They all uttered my name with a quite particular emphasis, as though it were not an honest, lawful name, but a nickname. And this infuriated me still more because I myself felt this ridiculous and totally unsuitable name to be a term both of contempt and derision; and that was so even during the days when it was still spoken with a certain amount of harmless respect. And thus in my young heart my feelings alternated with frenzied rapidity; I felt humiliated, yes, even debased, and immediately after—or rather, simultaneously—confident and proud, and sometimes all these feelings boiled up inside me together and fought against one another, a cruel torment, cruel in the heart of a small boy.

It was plain to see that the strong kind hand of the Prince protected me. Unlike all the other boys in our village, I was transferred to the higher school at D. just after I had reached the age of eleven. By many tokens I soon saw that the teachers there, too, knew the secret of my birth, and I was not a little pleased at that. But I never ceased to worry about my ridiculous name. I shot up like a cabbage stalk, and I grew broad in proportion, and my name was still Golubchik.

The older I became, the more I worried about this. I was a Krapotkin, and, by God, I had the right to call myself Krapotkin. But I determined to wait yet awhile. A year, perhaps. Perhaps the Prince would consider the matter in the meantime, and one day he would come over and, preferably in the presence of everybody, would bestow upon me his name, his title, and all his fabulous possessions. I made up my mind not to disgrace him. I studied hard and perseveringly. My teachers were well pleased with me. And yet all that, my friends, was not genuine ambition, it was only my devilish vanity which drove me on, and nothing else. Soon that fearful quality was to begin to work even more strongly within me. Soon I was to embark upon my first, although not yet despicable, undertaking. And that you shall hear about immediately.

•   •   •

Well, I had made up my mind to wait for a whole year, although, shortly after this decision, I began to think that a whole year was far too long a time. I soon tried to cut off a few months, for I was tortured with impatience. But at the same time I said to myself that a man who has decided to rise high in the world—and such a man I then considered myself to be—would indeed be unworthy if he showed impatience and weakened in his decisions. I also found a prop for my resolution in the superstitious conviction that the Prince in some secret, almost magical way must have long felt what I required of him. For I sometimes persuaded myself into thinking that I was possessed of magical powers and that by means of these I was in perpetual communication with my real father, even over a distance of many thousand versts. This conceit calmed me and held my impatience in check. But when the year was past, I held myself doubly justified in reminding the Prince of his duties towards me. And the fact that I had waited a whole year I naturally counted as no small credit to myself. Besides, something soon happened which seemed to prove clearly that even providence favored my plan. It was shortly after Easter, and well on into spring. At that time of the year I always felt—and still feel today—a new strength in my heart and muscles and a powerful, mad, unjustified conviction that I could succeed in even the most impossible undertakings. And there then occurred a most remarkable coincidence; for one day, in my lodgings, I chanced to overhear a conversation which was being carried on between my landlord and a strange man whom I could not see. At that time I would have given much to have been able to see the man and speak with him myself. But I dared not betray my presence. Obviously they believed that I was not at home, or at any rate not in my room. Indeed, they could never have guessed that I would be in the house at that hour, and I had only gone into my room by chance. My landlord, a postal official, was standing in the passage, conversing fairly loudly with the stranger. After the first few words, which I missed, I immediately realized that the stranger must be the man entrusted by the Prince with the duty of settling the monthly payment for my board, lodging, and clothing. Plainly my landlord had demanded an

increase in prices, and the emissary of the Prince was refus-
ing to agree to them. "But I tell you," I heard the stranger
say, "I cannot get in touch with him for another month. He
is in Odessa. He is staying there for seven or eight weeks.
He does not wish to be disturbed. He never opens a letter.
He is quite cut off from the world. He stares all day long at
the sea and cares for nothing. I tell you again: I cannot get
in touch with him."

"Well, how long must I wait, my friend?" said my landlord. "Since the boy's been here I've given him thirty-six
rubles extra pocket money; once he was ill, and the doctor
came six times. I have never been paid for that."
Incidentally, I knew that my landlord was lying. I had never
been ill. But I naturally paid no heed to that. What excited
me beyond all bounds was the inconsequent fact that
Krapotkin was living in Odessa, in a lonely house on the
seashore. A great storm arose in my heart. The sea, the
lonely house, the desire of the Prince to be cut off from the
world for seven or eight weeks: all that wounded me
deeply. It was as though the Prince had withdrawn from
the world only in order that he should hear no more of
me, and as though, in the whole world, he feared me
and only me.

So that's how it is, I said to myself. A year ago he
learned, by the magical way, of my decision. From under-
standable weakness he has done nothing. And now, since
the year is up, he is afraid of me and has gone into hiding.
But, my friends, so that you may understand my character

completely, I must add that I was at that moment even capable of a slight feeling of magnanimity towards the Prince. For I began to feel sorry for him. I was inclined to regard his flight from me as a pardonable weakness. So fantastically did I overestimate my powers. If my whole mad plan of bringing force to bear on the Prince was a ridiculous self-delusion, then the childish magnanimity with which I forgave him his weakness was certainly the product of a diseased mind, or as the doctors would call it, "a psychotic condition."

An hour after the aforementioned conversation, I started off to visit my mother, taking with me what remained of the money I had earned by giving lessons. When I now saw her again—she was terrified when I burst into the house so suddenly— I immediately perceived that she looked ill and aged. During the few months since I was last there her hair had turned gray. That frightened me. For the first time I saw on the person who was nearest to me in the world the signs of remorseless old age. And because I was still young, old age meant to me nothing less than death. Yes, death had already smoothed my mother's hair with his fearful hands, making it faded and silvery. So she would soon die, I thought, genuinely upset. And the guilt for that, I went on to think, lies on the shoulders of Prince Krapotkin. For, naturally enough, I was anxious to make out the Prince to be even guiltier than he already was in my eyes. The guiltier he was, the more righteous and justified appeared my project.

So I told my mother that I had only come for a few hours to tell her of a most remarkable and secret affair. The next day I was to go to Odessa. Nothing less had happened than that the Prince had summoned me to him. The news had been brought to me yesterday by an emissary of the Prince's who had called at my landlord's. She, my mother, was the only person to whom I had told a word of this. So she would please say nothing about it, I insisted stupidly and importantly. I made it apparent that the Prince was possibly ill and on the point of death.

But I had scarcely made this deceitful suggestion than my mother, who had been listening calmly, sitting on the wooden threshold of the house, sprang up. Blood rushed to her cheeks, tears welled out of her eyes; first she flung her arms out and then she clasped her hands together. I saw that I had frightened her, began to realize what she would say next, and myself fell into a cold terror. "Then I must go with you!" she said. "Come, quickly, quickly, he must not die, he must not die, I must see him, I must see him!" So great, so noble, I would like to say, was the love of this simple woman who was my mother. Many years had passed since she had felt the last kiss of her lover, but on her cheek she could feel the kiss as vividly as if it had been given only yesterday. Death itself had already touched her, but not even the touch of death could deaden or obliterate the touch of her lover. "Did he write to you?" asked my mother. "Be calm," I said. And since my mother could neither read nor write, I played an even more shameful deception upon her. "He wrote me a few lines in his own hand, so he cannot be very ill," I said.

In a moment she grew calm. She kissed me. And I was not ashamed to accept her kiss. She gave me twenty rubles, a fairly heavy little pile of silver wrapped up in a blue handkerchief. I hid it under my shirt above my belt.

Then I started out for Odessa.

• • •

Yes, my friends, I went to Odessa. I had a clear conscience, I felt no regret, I had my goal before my eyes and nothing should keep me from it. It was a brilliant spring day when I arrived. For the first time in my life, I saw a great city. It was no ordinary Russian city. Firstly it was a harbor; and secondly, most of the streets and parks were, as I had already heard, laid out in completely European style. Perhaps Odessa was not to be compared with Petersburg—that Petersburg which I carried in my imagination. But Odessa, too, was a great, an enormous city. It lay on the sea. It had a harbor. And it was the first town to which I had traveled quite alone, on my own initiative, the first wonderful stage on my wonderful journey "to the top."

As I left the station, I felt for the money under my shirt. It was still there. I took a room in a little hotel near the harbor. In my opinion, it was essential to live as near as possible to the Prince. Since, as I had heard, he lived in a house "on the sea," I imagined that it must be somewhere in the neighborhood of the harbor. I never doubted for a moment that the Prince, as soon as he learned of my arrival, would press me to come and live with him. And from there I would not have far to go. I burned with curiosity to discover the whereabouts of his mysterious house. I assumed that everyone in Odessa would know where the Prince lived. But I did not dare ask the owner of my hotel. It was fear that prevented me from making such an open enquiry, and also a sort of stupid pompousness. For already I saw myself as a Prince Krapotkin, and I was subtly amused at the idea that I was staying at a far too cheap hotel, incognito, under the ridiculous name of Golubchik. So I decided that I would rather get the desired information from the nearest policeman.

But first I went down to the harbor. I wandered slowly through the crowded streets, pausing at every shop window, especially before those displaying bicycles or knives, and made various plans for future purchases. Tomorrow, or the day after, I would be able to buy anything that pleased me, even a new suit of school clothes. Thus I continued until I reached the harbor. The sea was deep blue, a hundred times bluer than the sky, and also more beautiful because one could touch it with one's hands. And like the intangible clouds that sailed across the heavens, there were tangible ships, also white, large and small, sailing in and out of the harbor. A great, an indescribable, enchantment filled my heart, and for an hour I even forgot the Prince. There were a number of boats in the harbor, swinging gently at anchor, and when I came near to them I could hear the tender tireless lapping of the blue water against the soft white wood and hard black iron. I saw the cranes, soaring through the air like great iron birds and vomiting their loads out of their brown-black jaws into the waiting boats. Each of you, my friends, knows what it is to catch sight of the sea and a busy harbor for the first time in one's life. But I will not weary you with long descriptions.

After a time I felt the pangs of hunger and went into a confectioner's. I had reached that age at which hunger drives one, not into a restaurant, but into a confectioner's shop. I ate my fill. I believe that my voracious appetite created quite a sensation. I devoured one iced cake after another, for I had money enough, in my purse, and drank two cups of heavily sugared chocolate. Just as I was about to leave, a man suddenly stepped over to my table and said something to me which I did not immediately catch. I believe I was very frightened at first. Only when the man went on speaking did I slowly begin to comprehend. Indeed, he spoke with a foreign accent. I saw immediately that he was not a Russian, and this fact alone banished my first feeling of fear and woke in me a kind of pride. I don't really know why. But it seems to me that we Russians often feel flattered when we are given the opportunity of meeting foreigners. And by "foreigners" we understand Europeans, those people who are supposed to have so much more intelligence than we, although they are of far less worth. It sometimes seems to us that God has favored the Europeans, although they do not believe in Him. But perhaps they do not believe in Him simply because He has given them so much. And so they become presumptuous and believe that they made the world themselves, and after all that they're dissatisfied with it, although, according to their idea, they're the ones who are responsible. Think for a moment—I thought to myself, as I watched the stranger—there must be something very special about you if a European comes and talks to you casually like that. He is much older, perhaps ten years older than you. So we'll be polite to him. We'll show him that we're an educated Russian from the high school and no ordinary peasant. . . .

So I studied the stranger. He was what is called a "fop." He was holding a smart soft Panama hat in one hand, such a hat as was certainly not to be obtained throughout the length and breadth of Russia, and also a yellow cane with a silver knob. He was wearing a yellowish jacket of tussore, white trousers with a blue pin-stripe, and yellow button boots. And instead of a belt, his delicate little stomach was encircled by a low double-breasted waistcoat, made of white pique material and held together by three wonderful glittering mother-of-pearl buttons. Extraordinarily fascinating was his plaited gold watch-chain, with its numerous delicate little appendages, a miniature revolver, a tiny knife, a toothpick and a minute cowbell, all of purest gold. As to the man's face, I can remember it exactly. He had thick black hair, parted in the middle, a low narrow brow, and a tiny little mustache, twirled upwards so that the ends crept right into his nostrils. His coloring was pale—pallid—what is sometimes called "interesting." At that time, the whole effect seemed to me very impressive, an elegant representative of European worlds. Probably, I said to myself, he would never have spoken like that to an ordinary Russian, such as the others sitting in this shop. But with the expert glance of the European he has obviously recognized in me something special, a still nameless, but nevertheless genuine prince.

"I see, sir," said the strange gentleman, "that you are a stranger here in Odessa. I am, too. I am not a Russian. So in a certain sense we are companions, companions of fortune—"

"I only arrived today," I said.

"And I a week ago!"

"Where do you come from?" I asked.

"I am a Hungarian, from Budapest," he answered. "Allow me to introduce myself. My name is Lakatos, Jenö Lakatos."

"But you speak very good Russian!"

"Learned, my friend, learned," said the Hungarian, at the same time tapping my shoulder with the knob of his cane. "We Hungarians have a great talent for languages."

It was unpleasant to feel his cane upon my shoulder, so I shook it off. He begged my pardon and smiled, and I could see his gleaming white, somewhat dangerous teeth and a little bit of red gum above. His black eyes sparkled. I had never seen a Hungarian before, but I had a very good idea of them after all I had read about them in history. I cannot say that what I had read had tended to fill me with any respect for these people, who in my opinion were even less European than we. They were Tartars who had sneaked into Europe and remained there. They were vassals of the Emperor of Austria, who valued them so little that he had once had to call the Russians to his help when they rebelled. Our Czar had helped the Austrian Emperor to suppress the rebellious Hungarians. And I would perhaps have had nothing more to do with this Herr Lakatos, had he not suddenly done something amazing, something which impressed me beyond belief. He drew out of the left pocket of his pique waistcoat a little flat bottle, sprinkled himself, his lapels, his hands and his broad blue-and-white-spotted cravat; and immediately such a sweet odor arose that I was almost stupefied. It was, as I then thought, an absolutely heavenly scent. I could not resist it. And when he suggested that we should go and have dinner together, I immediately got up and obeyed.

Take note, my friends, of how cruelly God treated me when he placed that perfumed Lakatos at the first crossroads which I had to pass on my way through life. Without this meeting, my life would have been completely different.

But Lakatos led me straight to Hell. He even scented the way.

•   •   •

So we went out together, Herr Lakatos and I. Only after we had been walking for some time, backwards and forwards through the streets, did I suddenly notice that my companion limped. He only limped very slightly, it was scarcely perceptible, in fact it was not really a limp but rather as though his left foot was drawing a little loop, an ornament, on the pavement. Never since have I seen such a graceful limp; it was not a defect, but rather a perfection, a work of art—and it was this very fact that frightened me. At that time, you must know, I was a sceptic and also immensely proud of my scepticism. It seemed to me very clever that I, in spite of my youth, should already know that the sky was made of blue air and contained no angels and no God. And although I had every need to believe in God and the angels, and although in reality I was very sorry that there was nothing but blue air to be seen in the sky and that all happenings on earth were the workings of blind chance, I could not forgo my arrogant knowledge and the pride with which it filled me; so much so that, in spite of my longing to pray to God, I was nevertheless compelled at the same time to pray to myself. But when I noticed this graceful, even ingratiating and kindly limp of my companion, I believed that I had suddenly discovered that he was an emissary from Hell, not a man, not a Hungarian, not Lakatos, and I simultaneously realized that my scepticism was far from complete, and that that madness which I had once called my "*Weltanschauung*" had suddenly, so to speak, sprung numerous leaks. For although I might have ceased believing in God, the fear of the Devil and a belief in him still played a large and lively part in my imagination. And had I even been able to sweep the seventh Heaven bare, I was quite incapable of ridding Hell of all its terrors. There was no doubt that Lakatos limped, but at first I tried desperately to persuade myself that this was not so, to deny my eyes what they saw so plainly. Subsequently I said to myself that of course ordinary people can limp, and I called to mind all the people I knew who limped: our postman Vassili Kolohin, for example, and the woodcutter Melaniuk, and the innkeeper Stefan Olepszuk. But the more clearly I remembered all the limping men I had known, the plainer it became to me that there was a difference between their deformity and that of my new friend. Sometimes, when I thought he would not notice it, I carelessly dropped back a few steps and watched him. No, there was no doubt at all, he really did limp. Seen from behind, his walk was more extraordinary, more unusual, more illusive than ever; it was exactly as though his left foot drew invisible circular patterns on the ground, and his left button-boot, yellow, pointed, and extremely elegant, suddenly seemed to me—but for a second only—to be considerably longer than the right. At last I could stand it no longer, and in order to prove to myself that I had again suffered a so-called "relapse" into my old "superstition," I determined to ask Herr Lakatos whether he really limped. But I went about it very carefully, considering the wording of the question for a while, and then said: "Have you injured your left foot, or is your boot hurting you? It seemed to me that you were limping slightly." Lakatos stopped suddenly, gripped my sleeve so tight that I had to stop too, and said: "Fancy you noticing that! I must say, my young friend, you've got eyes like a hawk. No. Really. You have remarkably sharp eyes. Very few people have noticed that. But I can tell you about it. We haven't known each other long, but I already feel quite like an old friend, like an elder brother, if I may say so. Well, I have not injured my foot, and the boot fits perfectly. But I was born like that, I have limped ever since I started to walk, and as the years went by I even began to turn my deformity into a sort of art. I learned to ride and fence and play tennis. I can walk for hours and even climb. And I can swim and bicycle as well as anyone. You know, my friend, nature is never kinder than when she bestows some small deformity upon us. If I had come into the world perfect, I should probably have learned nothing."

While Lakatos said all this, he was holding me, as I have already mentioned, fast by the sleeve. He stood leaning against the wall of a house, with me opposite him, almost in the middle of the narrow pavement. It was a bright, pleasant evening. People strolled by us lazily and happily, the setting sun gilding their faces; the whole world seemed to me carefree and contented, only I was not—and that because I had to stay with Lakatos. At times I thought I must leave him in the next second, and yet it seemed to me as though he had a grip not only on my sleeve but also, to a certain extent, on my soul; as though he had discovered a tip of my soul and refused to let it go. At that time I could neither ride nor cycle, and suddenly it seemed to me shameful that I could do neither, although I was not a crip-ple. Well—my name was Golubchik, and that was worse than being a cripple for me, who was really a Krapotkin and had the right to ride the finest horses in the world. But that this Herr Lakatos was an adept at every sport, although he had been born with a limp; and that he was not even called Golubchik and was certainly not the son of a prince, made me feel quite particularly ashamed. Thus it came about that I, who had always borne my ridiculous name like a deformity, suddenly began to believe that it was this very name that would carry me to success, just as Herr Lakatos's lame foot had helped him to become an adept at sport. You can see, my friends, how the devil works. . . .

At the time I did not realize that, I only suspected it, but it was already more than a suspicion. It lay somewhere between a suspicion and a certainty. We walked on. "Now we will go and eat," said Lakatos, "and then you will come with me to my hotel. It's nicer, when one is in a strange town, to know that someone is with one, someone near, a good friend, a younger brother."

Well, we went and ate. We turned into the Tchornaya—and do you know where we went, my friends?

Here Golubchik paused. He looked at our host. The latter stared back at the narrator with his bright prominent eyes. At the word "Tchornaya" it seemed as though a light had been lit in his eyes, a quite extraordinary light. Yes, the "Tchornaya," he repeated. As I said—the "Tchornaya," began Golubchik again. At that time there was a restaurant there which bore exactly the same name as this one here, in which we are now sitting. It was called the "Tari-Bari"—and the owner was the same.

Our host, who was sitting opposite the speaker, now stood up, went around the table, spread out his arms, and embraced Golubchik. They drank eternal friendship; and all of us, too, his listeners, lifted our glasses and emptied them.

Well, that was where we went, began Golubchik again. Our host here, my friends, inaugurated, so to speak, my misfortune in his restaurant. For there were gypsies there, in the old "Tari-Bari" in Odessa, women who were marvelous violin and tambourine players. And what wines! And Herr Lakatos paid for everything. And I was in such a place for the first time in my life. "Drink up, drink up!" said Herr Lakatos. And I drank.

"Drink!" he repeated. And I drank again.

After a time, it must have been late in the evening, perhaps long after midnight—but in my memory it seems to me as though that whole night was one long midnight—

Lakatos asked me: "What are you actually doing here in Odessa?"

"I have come," I said (though I probably mumbled it at the time), "to visit my real father. He has been expecting me for several weeks."

"And who is your father?" asked Lakatos.

"Prince Krapotkin."

At this Lakatos banged his fork on his glass and ordered another bottle of champagne. I saw how he rubbed his hands under the table, and how above, across the table, across the white tablecloth, his narrow face lit up, suddenly reddened and grew fuller, as though he had puffed out his cheeks.

"I know him—His Highness, I mean," began Lakatos. "Now I understand what it's all about. He's a sly old fox, your papa! Of course, you are his illegitimate son! God help you, if you make even the smallest mistake! You must look as though you are strong and dangerous. He is as sly as a fox and as cowardly as a jackal! Yes, my son, you are not the first, nor are you the only one. There are probably hundreds of his illegitimate sons wandering about Russia. I know him. I've done business with him. Hops! I should have told you, I am a hop merchant. Well, go to his house tomorrow and announce yourself as Golubchik—see? And if they ask you what you've got to say to the Prince, simply tell them: Private business. And when you are standing inside, in front of his great black desk that looks like a coffin, and he asks you: 'What do you want?' you must say: 'I am your son, Prince!'—'Prince,' you must say. Not: 'Your

Highness.' And then you will see what happens. You must rely on your own wit after that. I will take you there. And I shall wait for you outside. And if he is at all unfriendly to you, just tell him that we have ways and means. And that you have a powerful friend! Understand?"

I understood all this very well, it ran like honey into my head, and I pressed Herr Lakatos's hand under the table, firmly and gratefully. He beckoned one of the gypsy women, then a second, and a third. Perhaps there were even more. For one of them at any rate, the one who came and sat beside me, I fell completely. My hand was caught in her lap like a fly in a net. Everything was hot, confused, senseless, and yet I felt exultantly happy.

I can still remember the gray, leaden morning, something soft and warm in a strange bed, in a strange room, shrill bells in the corridor outside, and most of all can I remember the shaming, shameless misery of a new day.

When I awoke, the sun was already high in the sky. As I went down the steps, someone said to me that the room had been paid for. From Lakatos I found only a note: "Good luck!" it said—and: "I have had to leave suddenly. Go by yourself. My best wishes are with you!"

So I went alone to the Prince's house.

•   •   •

The house of my father, Prince Krapotkin, stood solitary, proud and white on the outskirts of the city. Although a broad, yellow, well-kept road separated it from the shore, it seemed to me that day as though the house lay on the very edge of the sea. So blue and omnipotent was the sea on that morning when I approached the Prince's house that it looked as though its gentle waves were lapping continually over the stone steps of the house, only to withdraw at intervals to leave the road free. In addition to this, a board stood at the side of the road, long before one reached the house, which announced that vehicles were forbidden to proceed farther. It was obvious that the Prince did not wish his serene summer quiet to be disturbed. Two policemen were standing near the board, and they watched me while I stared at them as coolly and haughtily as if I myself had ordered their presence. If they had asked me what I was doing there, I would have answered that I was the young Prince Krapotkin. Actually, I was waiting for this question. But they let me pass, only following me a while with their glances; I could feel their eyes on the back of my neck. The nearer I approached Krapotkin's house, the more uneasy I became. Lakatos had promised to accompany me so far. Now I had only his note in my pocket. Loudly and vividly his words echoed in my head: "Don't call him Your Highness—say, Prince! He is as sly as a fox and as cowardly as a jackal!" Ever slower and more dragging grew my steps, and all at once I noticed the fearful heat of the day, which was approaching its zenith. The sky was blue, the sea on my right was motionless, and the sun beat down mercilessly upon my back. There was certainly thunder in the air, only it was not yet noticeable. I sat down for a little while at the side of the road. But when I stood up again I was even wearier than before. Very slowly, with a parching throat, I dragged my burning feet towards the white steps of the house. Blinding white they were, as white as milk and snow, and although they drank in the heat of the sun with every pore, they gave out a beneficent coolness. In front of the brown double-door stood an enormous doorkeeper, wearing a long sand-colored overcoat, a great black bearskin cap (in spite of the heat), and holding in one hand a large scepter on the end of which glittered a sort of golden apple. Slowly I climbed the flat stone steps. The doorkeeper did not seem to notice me until I stood immediately in front of him, small, perspiring, and very miserable. Even then, he did not move. Only his round blue eyes rested on me as on a worm, a snail, a nothing, as though I were not even human, like he, a being on two legs. Thus he stared at me for a while in silence. It was as though he did not ask my business simply because he knew already that such a miserable creature as I was quite incapable of human speech. Through my cap, through my skull, the sun burned fiercely, destroying the last few coherent thoughts that still buzzed in my head. Up till then I had really felt no fear or hesitation. But I simply had not reckoned with a doorkeeper, still less with one who never opened his mouth to ask me my business. So I still stood there, small and pitiful, in front of the yellow colossus and his menacing scepter. His eyes, which were as round as the ball on the end of his scepter, still rested on my despicable figure. I could think of no suitable question, my tongue lay dry, swollen, and cumbersome in my mouth. Then it suddenly occurred to me that he really ought to salute me or even take off his heavy cap; and rage boiled up in my breast at the thought of such impertinence from a lackey— a lackey in the service of my own father. I must order him—I thought rapidly—to take off his cap. But instead of giving this order, I took off my own cap to him and stood there, still more pitiful, bareheaded like a beggar. As though he had been waiting for just that, he now inquired, in an astonishingly thin, almost feminine voice, what my business was. "I wish to see the Prince," I said, very timorously and quite faintly. "Have you an appointment?" "The Prince is expecting me." "If you please," he said, somewhat louder and this time in a manly voice.

I entered. In the hall two lackeys, in sand-colored liveries and silver epaulettes and buttons, stood up from their chairs, arose as if by magic, as though they were stone lions such as one sees on the steps of lordly houses. I had again become master of myself and squeezed my beautiful cap in my left hand, which gave me a little more confidence. I said that I wished to see the Prince, he was expecting me, and it was private business. I was led into a little room, where hung a portrait of an old Krapotkin who, as I read on the little metal shield, was therefore my grandfather. I already felt quite at home, although my grandfather had a very unpleasant yellow haggard face. I am the blood of your blood! I thought. My grandfather! I'll show you who I am! I am not a Golubchik. I am yours. Or rather, you are mine!

Meanwhile I heard a soft silver bell ring, and a few minutes later the door opened and a servant bowed in front of me. I stood up. I went through the door. I was standing in the Prince's room.

The Prince could not have got up so very long before. He was sitting behind his great black writing desk, which really did look like a coffin in which Czars are buried, dressed in a soft, silver-gray, woollen dressing gown.

His face had only remained vaguely in my memory; now I had a chance to observe it. It was as though I saw the Prince for the first time in my life, and this realization gave me an unpleasant shock. It was, to a certain extent, as though this man were no longer my father, not the father for whom I had been prepared, but really a strange Prince, Prince Krapotkin indeed. He seemed to me grayer, thinner, drier, and taller than me, although he was sitting, while I stood before him. When he asked: "What do you want?" I lost my tongue completely. He repeated again: "What do you want of me?" Even today I can hear his voice. It was hoarse and a little threatening; it was, so it seemed to me then, a sort of bark, as though the Prince were performing the duty of one of his watchdogs. In very fact, there suddenly appeared in the room, without either of the two doors which I had already noticed having been opened, a gigantic wolfhound. I don't know where he came from, perhaps he had been waiting behind the

Prince's enormous chair. The dog remained motionless, standing between myself and the desk, and I too stared at him fixedly and was unable to take my eyes off him, although I wanted to look at the Prince and only at the Prince. Suddenly the animal began to growl, and the Prince said: "Quiet, Slavka!" He himself growled very like the dog. "Well, what do you want, young man?" he asked for the third time.

I was still standing close beside the door. "Come closer," said Krapotkin.

I took a tiny, a miserably tiny, step forward and recovered my breath.

"I have come to claim my rights!"

"What rights?" asked the Prince.

"My rights as your son," I answered, quite softly.

For a short while there was silence. Then the Prince said: "Sit down, young man." And he pointed to a wide chair in front of his desk.

I sat down. That is, I was entrapped by that accursed chair. Its soft upholstery lured me and held me fast, like one of those carnivorous plants which entice unsuspecting insects and destroy them utterly. I remained sitting, powerless, and as I sat there I felt more ignominious than during the whole time I had been standing. I did not even dare to rest my hands on the arms of the chair. They sank, as though paralyzed, and dangled foolishly over the sides, and suddenly I felt them beginning to swing, gently and ridiculously, and I had not the strength to stop them or even to lift them up again. The sun shone on my right cheek, powerful and dazzling, so that I could only see the Prince with my left eye. But I let both eyes sink and determined to wait for him to speak.

He now lifted a little silver bell, and a servant came in. "Paper and pencil!" demanded Krapotkin. I never moved, my heart began to thump wildly, and my arms swung harder than ever. The dog stretched himself comfortably on the floor and began to snore.

The writing materials were brought, and the Prince commenced:

"Well. Your name?"

"Golubchik!" I replied.

"Birthplace?"

"Woroniaki."

"Your father?"

"Dead."

"His profession, I mean," said Krapotkin, "I was not enquiring after his health."

"He was a forester."

"Any other children?"

"No!"

"Where were you at school?"

"At D."

"Were your reports good?"

"Yes."

"Do you wish to continue studying?"

"Yes!"

"Have you considered any particular profession?"

"No."

"I see," said the Prince and pushed the paper and pencil away. He stood up. Now I could see under his dressing-gown a pair of brick-red trousers, made of Turkish silk, as it seemed to me, and on his feet a pair of Caucasian sandals embroidered with pearls. He looked exactly as I imagined a sultan would look. He walked towards me, gave the dog a kick, at which the animal moved growling out of his way. Then he stood immediately in front of me, and I could feel his hard intense glance strike my skull like a knife point.

"Stand up!" he said. I got up. He towered above me by a good two heads. He studied me for a long time. "Who told you that you were my son?" "No one, I have known it for a long time; I guessed it and then found out." "I see," said Prince Krapotkin. "And who told you that you had any claims on me?" "No one—I know that I have." "And what claims or rights have you?" "The right to be called that." "To be called what?" "To be called that," I repeated, not daring to speak the actual name: "To be called the same as you." "So you want to be called Krapotkin?" "Yes." "Listen to me, Golubchik," he said. "If you are really my son, I've made a very bad job of it. You are a fool, a complete fool." In his voice I sensed a jeer, but also, for the first time, a little kindliness. "You must yourself admit, young Golubchik, that you are a fool. Do you admit it?" "No!" "Well, then I will explain to you. Throughout Russia I probably have many sons—who knows exactly how many? For many

years I was young, for far too long. Even you may already
have sons. I was at school once, too. My first son was by the
wife of the school porter, my second by the daughter of that
same porter. The first of those two sons is a legitimate
Kolohin, the second an illegitimate Kolohin. The names of
those two I can remember, because they were the first. But
my forester Golubchik I had completely forgotten, like so
many others . . . like so many others. And there obviously
cannot be a hundred Krapotkins running about the world,
eh? And by what right and what law do you all make these
claims? Even if there were a law dealing with that point,
what guarantee have I that they really are my sons. Eh? And
yet I look after them all, as far as my private exchequer is
aware of them. But since I am strict about being methodi-
cal, I have handed all these addresses over to my secretaries.
And now? Have you anything else to say?"

"Yes!" I said.

"Well, what, young man?"

Now I could observe the Prince quite composedly. I
was calm enough now, and when our type grows calm it
also grows cheeky and impertinent, and so I said: "I don't
care a straw for my brothers. All I'm concerned with is getting my own rights."

"What rights? You have no rights. Go home. Give
your mother my respects. Work hard. And become a useful citizen!"

I showed no signs of going away. I began again, obsti-
nately and rudely: "Once when you were in Woroniaki,

you carved me a little man out of wood, and then—"
I was about to speak of his hands, which had been so hard
and thin and had stroked my head so paternally—when
suddenly the door flew open, the dog jumped up and
began to bark joyfully, and the face of the Prince cleared
suddenly and lit up. A young man, scarcely older than I,
sprang into the room. The Prince opened his arms and
kissed the boy several times on both cheeks. Then at last
there was silence. The dog was still waving his tail. And suddenly the boy noticed me. "Herr Golubchik," said the
Prince, "my son!"

His son smiled at me. He had gleaming teeth, a wide
mouth, a yellowish complexion, and a fine, hard nose. He
did not look at all like the Prince, less like him than I, I
thought at the time.

"Well, good-bye," said the Prince to me. "Work hard."
He held out his hand. But then he drew it back and said:
"Wait!" and walked over to his writing desk. He pulled
open a drawer and took out of it a heavy gold snuffbox.
"Here," he said, "take this as a memento. God be with
you!"

He forgot to give me his hand. I never even thanked
him. I simply took the box, bowed, and left the house.

•   •   •

But scarcely was I outside and past the doorkeeper, to
whom I even said "Good-bye," in a daze of confusion and

fear, and who did not even answer me with so much as a glance, than I immediately began to feel that a great wrong had been done me. The sun stood already at noon. I felt hungry—and was curiously ashamed of that feeling; it seemed to me low and vulgar and unworthy of me. I had been wronged, and lo and behold, I only felt hungry. So perhaps I really was a Golubchik, nothing more than a Golubchik.

I walked back over the sunlit, sandy road, along which I had come scarcely two hours before. I literally hung my head, for I had a feeling as if it could never be held up again; it was heavy and swollen, as though it had been beaten —my poor head. The two policemen were still standing at the same spot. Now, too, they stared after me for a long time. Some while after I had passed them, I heard a shrill whistle. It came from the left, from the seashore, and it frightened me, although it roused me somewhat from my stupor. I raised my head and saw my friend Lakatos. Blithely he stood there, his yellow coat glistening gaily in the sun, his little cane waving at me, his smart panama hat lying beside him on the beach. At that moment he picked it up and began walking towards me. Blithely and without any perceptible effort he mounted the steep slope, which at this point separated the road from the sea, and in a few minutes he was standing beside me, offering me his smooth hand.

Only then did I notice that I was still holding the Prince's snuffbox in my right hand, and I pushed it, as adroitly as I could, into my pocket. But, quickly as I had made the movement, it had not escaped my friend Lakatos; I could see that from his look and his smile. At first he said nothing. He only tripped happily along beside me. Then, when the first houses of the town appeared before us, he asked: "Well, you were successful, I hope?" "Nothing was successful," I answered, and I was filled with a great rage against Lakatos. "If you had come with me," I went on, "as you promised yesterday, everything would have been quite different. You lied to me! Why did you write that you had to go away? Why are you still here?" "What!" shouted Lakatos, "do you think I've got nothing better to do than look after you. Do you think I'm going to bother myself with your miserable affairs? I received a telegram last night, calling me away. But it turned out later that there was no need for me to go. So I stayed, and came along here to enquire, as a good friend, how you had got on." "Well," I said, "I did not get on—in fact, I am not as far forward as I was." "So he wouldn't own you?" "No." "He gave you his hand?" "Yes," I lied. "And what else?" I pulled the snuffbox out of my pocket. I held it in the palm of my outstretched hand, stood still, and let Lakatos observe it. He did not touch it, he only ran his eye over it carefully. At the same time he clicked his tongue, pursed his lips, whistled a few notes, hopped a step forward and then back again, and at last said: "A marvelous piece. Worth a fortune. May I hold it?" And already he was stroking the box with the tips of his fingers. We had, by now, reached the town, and a few people were coming towards us. Lakatos whispered hastily: "Put it away!" and I hid the box.

"Well, was he alone, the old fox?" asked Lakatos. "No," I said, "his son came into the room." "*His* son?" said Lakatos. "He hasn't got one—I'll tell you something I forgot to warn you about last night. That boy is not his son. He is the son of Count P., a Frenchman. Ever since the boy was born, the Countess has been living in France; exiled so to speak. She had to give up her son. That's how it is. The old man must have an heir some time. Otherwise, who is to keep his fortune together? You, perhaps? Or I?"

"Do you know that for certain?" I asked, and my heart began to beat madly, with malicious joy, with a thirst for revenge; and suddenly I felt a burning hatred for this youth and a complete indifference towards the old Prince. All my feelings, my desires, my wishes, had suddenly found an object; once more I was filled with a new determination; I forgot that I had just received a bitter rebuff—or rather I thought I knew who alone was responsible for that rebuff. If—so I thought at the time— that youth had not entered the room, I could assuredly have won the Prince over to my cause. But that boy must have been warned, he must have known who I was, and that was why he had burst in so suddenly. The Prince had grown old and foolish, he had been artfully caught by this false son of his, this Frenchman, this child of a worthless mother.

It seemed to me then, while my thoughts ran on these lines, as though everything were growing clearer and brighter; the fire of hate was warming my heart. I believed that I had at last found the meaning of my life, and its object. The tragedy of my life was to be found in the fact that I was the wretched victim of a designing youth. The object of my life consisted, from that hour on, in my duty to destroy that same designing youth. An overwhelming feeling of gratitude to Lakatos filled me and compelled me to grip his hand, fast and firmly. He did not let my hand go. And thus we walked, almost like two children, hand in hand, towards the nearest restaurant. We ate plentifully, with robust appetites. Neither of us spoke much. Lakatos pulled a newspaper out of his coat pocket; it was like a conjuring trick, I had not noticed the paper until then. When we had finished eating, he called for the bill, pushed it towards me, and, still immersed in his paper, said quite casually: "You pay. We'll reckon up afterwards."

I put my hand in my pocket, pulled out my purse, opened it—and saw that it was filled entirely with copper coins instead of the silver which I had brought with me. I searched further in the middle compartment, remembering clearly the two ten-ruble pieces which I had put in there. For a few seconds longer I fumbled inside, and then terror overcame me and a dew of perspiration burst out on my forehead. Last night my money had been stolen from me, that was it.

Meanwhile Lakatos had begun to fold up his paper.

Then he asked: "Shall we go?" He looked at me and seemed to receive a sudden shock. "What's the matter?" he said. "I haven't any money left," I whispered.

He took the purse out of my hand, looked inside it, and at last said: "Yes, it was the women."

Then he pulled some money out of his notecase, paid, took me by the arm, and began: "That doesn't matter; it really doesn't matter, young man. We're far from desperate yet, we have a fortune in our pocket. That will fetch three hundred rubles among friends. And we'll stroll along to these friends now. And after that, my young friend, you'll have had enough adventures for the time being. Go straight home!"

Arm in arm I walked with Lakatos to visit the friends of whom he had spoken.

• • •

We went down into the quarter bordering the harbor, where the poorer Jews lived in tiny, tumbledown houses. I believe, by the way, that those people are the poorest and yet the most industrious Jews in the world. All day long they work in the harbor, toiling like machines, carrying cargoes aboard and attending to the ladings, and the weaker among them deal in fruits, pumpkins, pocket watches, clothes, repairing shoes, patching old trousers, and—well, they do everything that every poor Jew has to do. But they celebrate their Sabbath, from Friday evening—and Lakatos said: "We must hurry, for it's Friday today and the Jews will soon be shutting up their shops." As I hastened along by Lakatos's side, a great fear overcame me, and suddenly it seemed to me that the snuffbox which I was now on my way to sell did not belong to me at all; that Krapotkin had never given it to me, but that I had stolen it. However, I stifled that fear and even assumed a gay expression and behaved as though I had already forgotten that my money had been stolen from me, and I laughed at every anecdote that Lakatos told, although I heard not a word of what he said. I simply waited until he giggled, and then I knew that the story was finished and thereupon laughed loudly. I only realized vaguely that the stories were sometimes about women, sometimes about Jews, and sometimes about Ukrainians.

At last we stopped in front of a dilapidated hut belonging to a watchmaker. There was no sign outside; one could only tell from the little cogwheels and hands and watch-faces lying in the window that the inhabitant of the hut was a watchmaker. He was a tiny, dried-up Jew with a wispy little goatee beard. When he got up and came towards us, I noticed that he limped; his limp, too, was a tripping, delicate movement, almost like that of my friend Lakatos, only not quite so graceful and artistic. The Jew looked like a sad and somewhat overworked goat. In his little black eyes glowed a red fire. He took the snuffbox in his hand, weighed it for a moment, and then said: "Aha, Krapotkin!" At the same time he surveyed me with a rapid glance, and it was as though he were weighing me with his little eyes, just as he had weighed the box in his meager hand. Suddenly it occurred to me that the watchmaker and Lakatos were brothers, although they addressed one another quite formally.

"Well, how much?" asked Lakatos.

"The same as usual," said the Jew.

"Three hundred?"

"Two hundred."

"Two hundred and eighty?"

"Two hundred."

"We'll go!" said Lakatos and took the box from the watchmaker's outstretched hand.

We went a few houses further, and there again was a watchmaker's window, just the same as before; and lo and behold, when we entered the shop the same scrawny Jew with the goatee beard stood up. But he remained behind the counter this time, so I could not see whether he also limped. When Lakatos showed him my box, this second watchmaker also said only one word: "Krapotkin!" "How much?" asked Lakatos. "Two hundred and fifty," said the watchmaker. "Done!" said Lakatos. And the Jew paid us the money, in golden ten- and five-ruble pieces.

We left the harbor. "Well, young man," began Lakatos, "now we will take a cab and drive to the station. Be more sensible in future, don't get any more stupid ideas into your head, and keep tight hold of your money. Write to me sometime, to Budapest, here is my address." And he gave me his card, on which was written in Roman, as well as in Cyrillic letters:

JENÖ LAKATOS
Hop Merchant
Messrs. Heidegger & Cohnstamm, SAAZ,
Budapest Rakocziutca, 31.

It annoyed me that he should speak to me so condescendingly, and so I said: "I am very grateful to you, and also for the money."

"Don't thank me!" he answered.

"Well, how much was it?" I asked.

"Ten rubles," he said, and I gave him a gold ten-ruble piece.

Then he signaled a cab. We got in and drove to the station.

We had not much time to spare, for the train went in ten minutes, and the bell had already rung once.

I was about to get into the carriage when suddenly two very large men loomed up to the left and right of my friend Lakatos. They beckoned to me, and I climbed down. Then they closed in on either side of us and, sinister and threatening, led us along the platform. Not one of us spoke a word. We went round the great station building and then out at the back, where we could hear the whistlings of the shunting engines, and finally we turned into a little side door. Here was the police bureau. Two policemen were standing just inside the door. An official sat at a table in the middle of the room, occupying himself by trying to catch the numerous bluebottles which were flying about the room with a loud, incessant, penetrating buzz, and which persisted in settling every moment on the outspread sheets of white paper that lay scattered over the desk. Whenever the man caught a fly, he would take it between the thumb and first fingers of his left hand and pluck its wings off. Then he would drown it in his enormous ink-stained porcelain ink pot. Thus he left us standing for about a quarter of an hour—Lakatos and I and the two men who had brought us there. It was hot and still. The only sounds were the whistles of the locomotives, the buzzing of the flies, and the heavy, grunting breathing of the policemen.

At last the official beckoned to me. He dipped his pen into the inkpot, in which there were dozens of dead flies floating, and then asked me my name, my past history, and the purpose of my visit to Odessa. And after I had answered all that, he leaned back, stroked his beautiful blond beard, and bent suddenly forward again. "'How many snuffboxes did you really steal?" he asked.

I did not understand his question and remained silent.

He pulled open a drawer and beckoned me to his side. I walked round the table to the open drawer and saw that it was entirely full of snuffboxes, all exactly like the one I had received from the Prince. I stood in front of that drawer, rooted with horror. I could understand nothing more. I felt as though I had been bewitched. Dazedly I drew out of my pocket the ticket which I had bought half an hour before, and showed it to the official. It was ridiculous to do such a thing, I realized it immediately, but I was helpless, confused, and, like everyone who is confused, I felt that I must do something, however senseless. "How many of these boxes did you take?" asked the man once more.

"One," I said. "The Prince gave it to me. This gentleman knows that." I pointed to Lakatos. He nodded. But at that moment the official shouted: "Out!" and Lakatos was led away.

I was now alone with the official and one policeman, who was still standing by the door. The latter, however, seemed not to be alive, he was more like a post or some other incriminate object.

The official dipped his pen again into the ink pot, fished out a dead and dripping fly—it looked as though the fly were bleeding ink—watched it for a moment, and then said quietly: "Are you the Prince's son?"

"Yes!"

"You wanted to kill him?"

"Kill him?" I asked.

"Yes," said the official, quite softly and smiling.

"No, no!" I shouted. "I love him."

"You may go," he said to me. I walked across to the door. Suddenly the policeman gripped my arm. He led me out. There stood a police van with barred windows. The door of the van opened. Inside sat another policeman who pulled me in. We drove off to prison.

* * *

Here Golubchik made a long pause. His mustache, whose lower edge had become moist with the schnapps which he had been drinking in great draughts, trembled slightly. The faces of all his listeners were pale and immobile and had, so it seemed to me, grown richer in wrinkles and lines, as though each of those present had, during the hour since the commencement of the story, lived both his own youth and that of Semjon Golubchik. Now there rested on us the burden, not only of our own lives, but also of that part of Golubchik's life which he had just related to us. And it was not without a certain alarm that I awaited the rest of this man's story, which to a certain extent, I should have to experience rather than hear. Through the closed door one could already hear the rumbling of the first vegetable carts on their way to market, and sometimes the mournful, long-drawn whistle of distant trains.

It was only an ordinary police arrest, began Golubchik again, nothing terrible. I was put into a fairly comfortable room, with wide grills across the high windows, grills as little menacing as the bars across the windows of many houses. In the room there was a table, a chair, and two camp beds. But the terrible thing was that, as I entered the room, my friend Lakatos got up from one of the beds and greeted me. Yes, he offered me his hand just as gaily and nonchalantly as if we had met, for example, in a restaurant. But I ignored his outstretched hand. He sighed, with a sorrowful and injured air, and lay down again. I sat on the chair. I wanted to cry, to lay my head on the table and cry, but I was ashamed of doing so in front of Lakatos, and still stronger than my shame was my fear that he might try to comfort me. So I sat there, with a sort of stony sobbing in my breast, silent upon the chair, and counted the bars outside the window.

"Don't be downcast, young man!" said Lakatos after a while.

He stood up and walked over to the table. "I have found out all about this." Against my will, I raised my head, but regretted the move immediately. "I have my connections, even here already. In two hours at the very latest you will be free, And do you know whom we have to thank for this misfortune? Do you know? Go on—guess!"

"Tell me!" I shouted. "Don't torture me!"

"Well, your fine brother—or rather, the son of Count P. Now do you understand?"

Oh, I understood, and yet I did not understand. But that hatred, my friends, the hatred for that young man, the bastard, the false son of my natural, my princely father, usurped the role of common sense—as so often happens; and because I hated, I thought I understood also. In a flash, so it seemed to me, I saw through a fearful plot that had been woven about me. And for the first time the desire for vengeance, that twin sister of hate, awoke within me; and even quicker than the thunder follows the lightning, I swore to myself that one day I would revenge myself on that boy. How—I knew not; but I already felt that Lakatos was the man to show me the way, and therefore in that instant I felt even attracted to him.

Of course, he knew everything that was passing in my mind. He smiled, and I recognized in his smile that he knew everything. He bent over the table, so near to me that I could see nothing but his gleaming teeth and, behind, the reddish glistening of his gums and from time to time the pink tip of his tongue, which reminded me of the tongue of our cat at home. In very fact, he knew everything. The situation was as follows: To give away boxes, all of the same extremely expensive sort, was one of the many caprices of the old Prince. He had them specially made for him by a jeweller in Venice, after the design of an old snuff-box which he, the Prince, had bought at an auction. These snuffboxes, which were made of solid gold inlaid with ivory and encircled with emerald chips, were presented by the Prince to his guests, and he always had dozens of them in the house. Well, the whole thing was simple. The young boy, whom he regarded as his son, needed money, stole the boxes, and sold them from time to time; and in the course of years the police, as the result of periodical visits paid to the shops round the harbor, had collected an enormous number of these boxes. All the world knew where these precious objects came from. Even the Prince's steward, even his lackeys, knew it. But who would have dared tell him?— How easy it was then to accuse an unimportant youth like myself of theft, of burglary even; for what was a person of our class in old Russia, my friends? An insect, one of those flies which the official had drowned in his ink pot, a nothing, a grain of dust under the heels of the great nobility. But, my friends, let me digress for a moment, and forgive me for keeping you here: I wish today that we were still the old grains of dust! Our lives were ordered not by laws but by whims. And yet even laws are dependent upon whims. For laws have to be interpreted. Laws, my friends, can never protect a man from arbitrary usage, for laws are dispensed by arbitrary men. What do I know of the whims of a little judge? They are worse than the whims of ordinary people. They are nothing but petty animosities. But the whims of a great nobleman I know. They are more constant even than laws. A real nobleman, who can both punish and pardon, is often incensed by a single word, but he can also be conciliated by a single word. And think how many great noblemen there have already been who were never harsh! Their whims were always kindly ones. But laws, my friends, are nearly always harsh. There can hardly be a single law of which one can say: it is a kindly one. Nowhere on earth is there absolute justice, for justice, my friends, is only to be found in Hell . . . !

But to return to my story. At that time I wished there were Hell on earth, for I thirsted after justice. And whoever desires absolute justice, has already fallen a victim to the lust for revenge. Such was I at that time. I was grateful to Lakatos for having opened my eyes. And I forced myself to trust him and asked him: "What must I do then?"

"Tell me first, between ourselves," he began, "had you really no other intention than to inform the Prince that you were his son?—You can tell me everything, no one can hear us. We are comrades in distress now, confidence for confidence. Who sent you to the Prince? Is there in your school class a member of the—well, you know what I mean—the so-called Revolutionary?"

"I don't understand you," I said. "I'm not a revolutionary. I simply want my rights! My rights!" I shouted.

Only much later was I to realize what sort of a part this Lakatos was playing. Only much later, when I myself had almost become a Lakatos. But at that time I realized nothing. He, however, had understood very well that I had spoken the truth. He only said: "Well, that's all right then." And he probably thought at the same time: Now I've made a mistake again; I've missed a nice sum of money there.

Some time later the door opened, and the official who had drowned the flies came in; following him was a man in civilian dress. I got up. The official said: "I'll leave you alone now," and went out. After him went Lakatos, without looking at me. The man said I was to sit down, he had a suggestion to make. He knew everything—so he began. The Prince held a high and important position in the country. On him depended the welfare of Russia, of the Czar, of the whole world, one might say. Nothing, therefore, must be allowed to truble him. I had gone to him with ridiculous demands. Only the gracious clemency of the Prince had saved me from a heavy punishment. I was young. Much could be excused me. But the Prince, who till now had been pleased to maintain the son of his forester and pay for his education, no longer wished to squander his kindnesses on an unworthy or unscrupulous or inconsiderate fool—on me, in fact, however I liked to describe myself. Consequently, it had been decided that I should be put into a job which would determine my future for me, now and forever. I could either become a forester like my father, with the prospect of some day being promoted to agent on one of the Prince's estates; or else I could enter the service of the State—the Post, Railways, as a clerk somewhere, in any Government office I liked. Well paid positions and well suited to me.

I answered nothing.

"Here, sign!" said the man and spread out in front of me a piece of paper on which was written that I had no claims of any sort on the Prince and that I undertook never to attempt to see him again.

Well, my friends, I cannot describe to you exactly my feelings at that moment. As I read that paper, I felt ashamed, humiliated, but also proud, simultaneously afraid and vengeful, hungry for freedom and at the same time ready to suffer torments, to carry a cross; filled with a craving for power and also with a sweet, seductive feeling that impotence was a matchless blessing. But above all I wanted to have power so that one day I might be able to avenge myself for all the insults which had been heaped upon me, and at the same time I wanted to have the strength to enable me to suffer these insults. In short, I wanted to be not only an avenger but also a martyr. As yet I was neither, I realized that well enough, and the man assuredly knew it also. He said to me, this time harshly: "Well, quick, make up your mind!" And I signed.

"Good," he said, and put the paper into his pocket. "Now, which do you choose?"

Would to God that I had then said what was on the tip of my tongue; namely the simple words: Home! To my mother! But at that moment the door opened and a police officer stepped in, a brilliant figure with a shining saber and a polished holster and a dazzling glance of fire and ice. And only because of him, and without looking at the other man, I said suddenly: "I want to join the police!"

Those thoughtless words, my friends, decided my fate. Only much later did I learn that words are mightier than deeds—and I often laugh when I hear the well-worn phrase: "Not words, but deeds!" How impotent deeds are! A word endures, a deed perishes! Even a dog can perform a deed, but only a man can speak a word. A deed, an action, is a phantom compared with the reality, even the abstract reality of a word. Action stands roughly in the same relation to words, as the two-dimensional shadow in the cinema to the three-dimensional living man, or, if you like it, as the photograph to the original. That, too, is the reason why I became a murderer. But that comes later.

Meanwhile, I signed another paper in the room of an

official whom I had not seen before. I cannot remember exactly what was in that second paper. The official was an elderly man with a beard so imposing, so long and so silvery, that his face above it seemed tiny and unimportant, as though the face had grown up from the beard and not the beard down from the face. When I had signed, he gave me his soft, fat, flabby hand and said: "I hope you will soon feel at home with us and grow accustomed to our ways. You will proceed now to Niijn-Novgorod. Here is the address at which you are to report. Good-bye!"

And just as I reached the door, he called out: "Stop!" I walked back to his desk. "Pay attention to this, young man," he said, now almost angrily. "Keep silent! Listen! Keep silent! Listen!" He laid his finger against his bearded lips and waved with his hand.

Thenceforward I was a member of the police—a member of the Ochrana, my friends! I began to forge plans for my revenge. I had power. I had hate. I was a good agent. After Lakatos I no longer dared to enquire. He will often reappear in my story. But spare me the details, which I ought now to tell you, of what I did during the next few years. There is enough that is horrible and repulsive in my life which must yet be related.

·   ·   ·

So, with your permission, I will omit any detailed account of the mean and loathsome things which I was forced to do during the years following my enlistment in the police. You all know what the Ochrana was. Some among you may even have suffered under it yourselves. In any case, there is no need for me to describe it to you. You know now what I became. And if that is too much for you to bear with, please say so, immediately, and I will go. Has anyone anything against me? Gentlemen, I beg of you to speak out. But quickly. And I will leave you.

But none of us spoke a word. Only our host said: "Semjon Semjonovitch, since you have already begun to tell your story, and since we all of us here have surely something on our consciences, I ask you, in the name of us all, to continue." Golubchik took another gulp from his glass and then resumed:

I was no fool, in spite of my youth, and so I was very soon regarded favorably by my superiors. But first—I forgot to tell you—I wrote a letter to my mother. I told her that the Prince had received me kindly and that he sent his respects to her. He had obtained for me—so I went on to write—a wonderful position in the employ of the State, and from now on I would send her ten rubles a month. There was no need for her to thank the Prince for this money.

When I wrote this letter, my friends, I knew already that I would never see my mother again, and I was also, strange as it may seem, very sad at the thought. But something else, something stronger—so it seemed to me at the time—was calling to me, stronger even than the love for my mother, and that something was the hatred I felt for my false brother. My hatred was as loud as a trumpet, and my love for my mother was as tender and soft as a harp. You will understand, my friends.

So I became, young as I was, a first-class agent. I cannot tell you all the despicable things which I did during that time. But some among you may still perhaps remember the case of the young Jewish Socialist revolutionary, Salomon Komrover, better known as Komorov. Well, that was one of the foulest thing I ever did in my life.

This Salomon Abramovitch Komrover was a youth from Kharkov. Politics had never held the slightest interest for him. As is befitting for a Jew, he studied the Talmud and the Torah diligently, hoping one day to become a sort of Rabbi. His sister, however, was a student; she studied philosophy in Petersburg, she mixed with the Socialist revolutionaries, she wished, as was the fashion at that time, to free the people—and one day she was arrested. Whereupon Salomon Komrover, her brother, went immediately to the police and announced that he, and he alone, was responsible for the dangerous activities of his sister. Good! He, too, was arrested. And during the night I was put into his cell. It was in a prison in Kiev. I can even remember the exact time—a few minutes before midnight. When I entered—that is, when I was thrown in—Salomon Komrover was pacing up and down; he seemed not to have noticed me. "Good evening," I said, and he did not answer me. I behaved, according to instructions, as though I were a hardened criminal and lay down with a sigh on my bed. After a time, Komrover, too, ceased to wander about and also went and sat on his bed. I was used to that. "Political?" I asked, as usual. "Yes!" he said. "How so?" I went on. Well, he was young and stupid, and he told me the whole story. But I, still thinking of my false brother, the young Prince Krapotkin, and of my revenge, wondered whether here, at last, was not the opportunity to cool my ever-burning hatred. And I began to persuade the unsuspecting young Komrover that I knew a way out for him and his sister. That was, that he should say that the young Prince was a friend of his sister's, and then, so I told the terrified youth, once a name like Krapotkin's had been brought into the case, there was nothing more to be feared.

Actually, I had no idea that the young Prince was really involved in revolutionary circles and that for a long time he had been kept under close observation by my colleagues. So my hatred and my desire for vengeance had one might say, met with a certain amount of luck. For hear what happened. A few days after the police had arrested Komrover, they brought into our cell a very handsome young man in the uniform of the Imperial Engineers. It was my false half-brother, the young Prince Krapotkin.

I greeted him, but of course he did not recognize me. With insidious persistence I began to worm my way into his confidence. Komrover, who lay on his bed in a corner, now held no more interest for me. And as Lakatos had once done with me, I began also to do with the Prince, luring information out of him, one thing after another, betrayal after betrayal; only with more success than Lakatos had had with me. Yes, I even asked the young Prince whether he still remembered the snuffboxes which his father used to give to his guests. That startled the young man; he reddened, I could see it even in the semi-darkness of the cell. That is just what happened: the man, who had perhaps plotted to overthrow the Czar, grew red when I reminded him of his boyhood escapades. From then on he willingly gave me all the information I asked. I learned that, as a direct result of that ridiculous affair with the snuffboxes, which had one day come to light, the youth had felt himself driven to adopt a hostile attitude towards law and order. Like so many young men of his time, he had used the fact that his vulgar little pilferings had been discovered as an excuse for becoming a so-called revolutionary and for attacking the existing organization of society. He was still handsome, and when he spoke, and even when he smiled with his white teeth, the gloomy cell in which we were imprisoned grew brighter. His uniform was faultless in cut. Faultless in shape, too, was his face, his mouth, his teeth, his eyes. I hated him.

He told me everything—everything, my friends! There is no longer any point in my telling you all that he said. But it did me no good when I reported our conversations. For punishment was meted out, not to the young Prince Krapotkin, but to the completely innocent Jew, Komrover.

I can still see how they came in and hammered the

chain and ball around his left leg. He went to Siberia. But the young Prince vanished one day, quicker than he had come.

Every statement that the Prince had made to me had been attributed to young Komrover.

Such was the practice in those days, my friends!

I was with him in the cell during his last night. He cried a little, gave me a few notes to his parents and friends and relations, and then said: "God is everywhere. I do not fear. Neither do I hate. No one! You were my friend and a friend in need. I thank you!"

He embraced me and kissed me. Still today his kiss burns on my face.

And at those words Golubchik raised a finger and stroked his right cheek.

•   •   •

Some time later I was transferred to St. Petersburg. You cannot know what such an appointment meant. In St. Petersburg one acted under the immediate orders of the most powerful man in Russia, the head of the Ochrana. On him depended the safety of the Czar himself. My superior was none less than Count W., a Pole; even today I dare not mention his name. He was an extraordinary man. Everyone of us who served under him had to take a special oath in his room. An enormous silver crucifix stood between two yellow wax-candles on his black desk. Black curtains

covered the doors and windows. Behind the desk, on a dis-
proportionately high black chair, sat the Count, a little man
with a bald head covered with freckles, with pale watery
eyes which reminded one of dried forget-me-nots, shriv-
elled ears like yellow papier mâché, prominent cheek-
bones, and a perpetually half-open mouth which revealed
his great strong teeth. This man knew everyone of us
employed in the Ochrana; he watched over our every step,
although he never seemed to leave his office. He seemed to
us uncanny, and we were far more afraid of him than the
country was of us. We had to swear a long oath in front of
him, in his mysterious room, and before we left him, he
said to each one of us: Now, beware! Child of Death! Is
your life dear to you? To which we answered: Yes,
Excellency!—and he dismissed us.

One day I was summoned by his secretary, who
informed me that there was a special job on hand for
myself and several of my companions. The great Parisian
dress-designer, Monsieur Charron—that was the first time
I had heard the name—had been invited to Petersburg. He
was proposing to give a display of his latest models in the
Petersburg Theater. Several grand dukes were interested in
the mannequins. Several ladies in the highest society were
interested in the dresses. Now arose the question—so said
the secretary—of arranging a special form of surveillance.
For who knew what undesirable characters there might
not be among Monsieur Charron's mannequins? Might
they not hide weapons or bombs under their clothes? And

how easy that would be for them! They would naturally have to change every five minutes, go from the stage to their dressing rooms and back again, and an accident might easily happen. Monsieur Charron had announced that he was bringing fifteen girls with him. So we needed fifteen men. The job might necessitate transgressing the ordinary laws of decency. But we would have to be prepared for that. Would I make all arrangements and take charge of the case, the secretary asked me?

This unusual, even fantastic duty pleased me greatly. I see now, my friends, that I cannot avoid making mention of even the most intimate things in my life. So I must confess to you that up till that time I had never been really in love, as is usually the case with young men. Except for the gypsy whom my friend Lakatos had introduced to me, my experiences with women had been limited to the few occasions on which I had possessed and paid for a girl in one of the so-called houses of pleasure. Although my profession necessitated my knowing the world and also gave me every opportunity of doing so, I was still young enough to imagine that I would simply have to watch these Parisian mannequins during the actual shows, and that I had been selected to spy upon these exquisite ladies in all their entrancing nakedness, and even, perhaps, to "possess" them. I immediately said that I was ready to take on the job and set about choosing my fourteen co-workers. They were the smartest and youngest fellows in our division.

The evening on which the Parisian dressmaker, together

with his mannequins and innumerable trunks, arrived in Petersburg, brought us no small amount of worry.

We arrived at the station, fifteen in number, and yet it seemed to each of us as though we were only five or even two. Our supreme chief had instructed us to be particularly on the alert; and all this simply because of a dressmaker. We mingled with the crowds who had come to meet their relatives at the station. At that time I was convinced that I had been entrusted with a particularly arduous and important duty. I had no less a task than, for all I knew, to save the life of the Czar.

.   .   .

When the train steamed in, and the world-famous dressmaker descended from his carriage, I saw immediately that our chief had made a mistake. This was not the sort of man who could be even remotely suspected of plotting an assassination. He looked well-fed, vain and harmless, and showed himself extremely anxious to attract the greatest possible amount of attention. To put it briefly: he was certainly not a "subversive individual." He was a fairly tall man, but in consequence of his curious attire he gave the impression of being smallish or even short. For his clothes flapped about him, instead of simply covering him, and they made no pretense of fitting, in fact they might have been presented to him by a casual acquaintance. But he had designed them himself and therefore he seemed to us, or to

me at any rate, to be, as one might say, doubly clothed. I
was amazed that the Czar's court could summon such a
ridiculous creature all the way from Paris to Petersburg;
and then, for the first time, I began to have doubts—doubts
as to the safety of the fine gentlemen, of the great noblemen, to whose company I would so gladly have belonged.
Up to that moment I had believed in their infallibility.
How, therefore, could they have invited to Petersburg such
a comedian as this, who was to dictate to their women-folk
what fashions were to be worn in Russia? It was incredible! But now I saw it with my own eyes. The dressmaker
arrived with a large retinue, and not only a feminine one,
such as we had expected. No!—he had also brought several young men with him, evidently the last word in Parisian
manhood, complete with silk cravats and abundant ges-
tures. They hopped gaily out of their compartments, not
unlike dressed-up sparrows—in fact the illusion would
have been complete had they suddenly started twittering.
To me, indeed, the noisy and light-hearted way in which
they began chattering among themselves as soon as they
had arrived seemed like a cheerful confabulation between
human birds or partially feathered humans.

They waited for a while outside the carriage, then
stretched out their arms and received the twelve girls
who began to emerge after them. They caught them so
carefully and delicately, and with such anxious faces, that
they might not have been simply stepping down on to a
platform but plunging into a fearful abyss. Among the

girls who got out, one in particular caught my attention.
Like all the girls whom the dressmaker had brought with
him, she was wearing a number. For each of them bore a
number, embroidered in red on a neat blue satin square,
which was pinned over the left breast. And it looked
exactly as though these numbers had been branded on, as
one brands horses or cattle. Although the girls were all so
merry, I felt extremely sorry for them; I pitied them all,
especially the one who had attracted me at first glance.
She bore the Number 9, and was called, as I discovered
later, Lutetia. But in the passports, which I shortly after
inspected in the passport office, her name was given as
Annette Leclair, and—I do not know why—this name
moved me deeply. Perhaps it is unnecessary to assure you
again that I had never really loved a woman before;
indeed, I had had very little to do with women. I was
young and well-built, and in no way indifferent to their
charms; but my heart was far from ready to obey my senses.
And strong as was my desire to "have" them nearly all, it
was more than counterbalanced by my conviction that I
could never be in a position to monopolize even one of
them. And yet, as must be the case with every young man,
I yearned for the one woman—or rather, for one of the
ones—who could forever satisfy my longings and still my
restless discontent. At the same time, I suspected that such
a woman could probably never exist, and yet I waited
anxiously—as is also the way with young men—for the
miracle to happen. And the moment I set eyes on Lutetia,

Number 9, it seemed to me that the miracle had indeed arrived. When a young man, such as I was then, is full of expectation, he is only too ready to believe that the desired object has entered his life.

So I fell in love with Lutetia, literally, at first sight. Very soon it seemed to me that she carried her number like a stigma, and suddenly I was filled with hatred against this exquisite dressmaker, who had been invited by the highest society to exhibit his unhappy slaves. Of all these unhappy slaves it was, of course, Lutetia, with her Number 9, who seemed to me the unhappiest. And as though this contemptible but far from criminal dressmaker were in reality a slave-trader or a white-slaver, I began considering the ways and means by which I might rescue Number 9 from his clutches. Yes, I saw in the fact that I had been sent to Petersburg on account of this wretch, a particular "gesture of fate." And I made up my mind to save Lutetia.

• • •

I believe I forgot to tell you why the police had taken these precautions against such an unusual, but nevertheless unsuspicious, dressmaker. A week or two previously an attempt had been made on the life of the Governor of Petersburg. As you all know, unsuccessful assassinations used to have far more terrible results in our old Russia than successful ones. Successful assassinations were, to a certain extent, the irrevocable will of God. For, my friends, people

still believed in God in those days, and they were convinced that nothing could happen against His will. But in
order to forestall, so to speak, the Almighty before he could
find an opportunity of destroying a high personage, so-
called precautionary measures were taken. These measures
were mostly hopeless and often ridiculous. We, for example, were given orders to watch those poor young girls
particularly closely during the intervals while they were
changing, and also during the daytime, in their hotels. We
were also ordered to take particular note of the men with
whom, in all probability, they would come in contact. And
so, during those days, we were really no longer policemen,
but a sort of group of governesses. I, however, was in no
way ashamed of this task, indeed it amused me. But what
would not have amused me during those first happy days
when I was in love!—My heart! I felt I had denied it up
till then. Ever since that moment when love had entered
in, I had realized that it was still there, my heart, and that,
up to that hour, I had only ignored, insulted and repressed
it. Or so I believed. Yes, my friends, it was an unspeakable
joy to feel that I still possessed a heart and to recognize my
crime in having previously ill-treated it. At the time I had
no such clear conception of my feelings as I have now. But
I already felt that love had begun to redeem me and that
the greatest gift it could bring me would be my redemption, with suffering, with joy, and even with pleasure. For
love, my friends, does not make us blind, as the stupid
proverb asserts. On the contrary, it makes us see. Suddenly,

and thanks to my foolish love for an ordinary girl, I realized that up to that hour I had been evil, and I realized, too, exactly how evil I had been. Since then, I have come to realize that the object which awakes love in a human heart is utterly unimportant compared to the knowledge which that love bestows. Whoever or whatever a man may love, his perception grows greater, not less. Yet I still did not know whether the girl would return my love. But the blessing of being able to fall in love so suddenly, at first sight, made me sure of myself and simultaneously aroused pangs of conscience within me at the shamefulness of past deeds. I tried to become worthy of this gift. In a flash I realized the baseness of my profession, and it disgusted me. At that time I began to make amends; it was the beginning of my period of atonement. Little did I know then how much more I should have to atone for later.

I watched the girl whom they called Lutetia. I watched her, no longer as a policeman, but as a jealous lover; no longer because of my duty, but because of my heart. And it gave me a quite particular pleasure to watch her and to know, every moment, that she was really in my power. So cruel, my friends, is human nature! For even when we realize that we have been vile, we still remain vile. We are men! Good and bad. Bad and good. Nothing more than men!

I suffered the tortures of Hell while I was watching that girl. I was madly jealous. Every moment I trembled lest another man, another of my colleagues, might perchance be ordered to take my place in guarding her. I was young then, my friends. And when a man is young it sometimes happens that jealousy comes with the beginning of love; and a man can be happy in the midst of his jealousy, even because of his jealousy. Suffering makes us just as happy as joy. Indeed, one can scarcely distinguish between suffering and joy. The real ability to draw that distinction only comes with age. And by then we are already too feeble to avoid suffering and appreciate joy.

·   ·   ·

In reality—or have I told you already—the name of my beloved was, of course, not Lutetia. It may seem pointless to you that I mention this, but to me it meant much that she had two names, a real one and a false one. For a long time I kept her passport in my pocket. I took it to police headquarters, copied down even the dates on it, had, as was customary with us, the photograph retaken, kept two prints for myself, and put them in a special envelope. Both names fascinated me, each in a different way. Both names I had heard for the first time. From her real name there emanated a warm, subtle glamour, from the name Lutetia a resplendent, imperious glitter. It was almost as though I loved two women instead of one, and, since they were one, as though I had to love that one twice as much.

During the evenings when the girls were in the theater, parading the dresses—or, as the newspapers called them, the "creations"—we had to stand on duty in the dressing rooms. Monsieur Charron made a furious protest against this. He went to the widow of General Portchakoff, who at that time was an important personage in Petersburg society and who had been the main instigator of his visit to Russia. In spite of her famous embonpoint the widow was extraordinarily impetuous. She possessed the astonishing ability of being able to visit, on the same morning, two archdukes, the governor-general, three lawyers, and the intendant of the Imperial opera, in order to protest against this decree of the police. But, my friends, of what use in old Russia, in circumstances such as these, was a protest against a decree? The Czar himself could have done nothing—he least of all, perhaps.

Of course, I was fully aware of all the activities of this energetic old woman. Indeed, I even paid out of my own salary for the sleigh which I hired in order to be able to follow her; and also out of my own pocket came the bribes which I gave to the servants and lackeys in return for detailed accounts of the conversations which took place in every house she visited. I did not fail immediately to report the results of my investigations to my chief. He congratulated me, but I was ashamed of his congratulations. For I was no longer working for the police. I was in the service of something higher; I was in the service of my passion.

In those days I was probably the smartest of all the secret agents. For I possessed not only the capacity of being quicker than the impetuous widow, but also the extraordinary gift of being in several different places almost simultaneously. Thus I was able to watch not only Lutetia, but also the general's widow and the dressmaker at one and the same time. There was only one thing I did not see, my friends, only one thing. And you will shortly hear what that was. One day, therefore, I saw the famous dressmaker come out of his house. He was wrapped in an enormous fur coat which he had had made in Paris—for it was not a real Russian coat, but only such a one as the Parisians think is worn in Russia. Round his shoulders was an effeminate little cape of astrakhan, and on his head a hood of blue fox with a silver tassel. He climbed into a sleigh and drove off to the general's widow. I followed, reached the house long before him, relieved him of his remarkable furs—for I was a friend of the footman's—and waited in the hall. The enterprising widow had disastrous news for him. I, too, succeeded in listening to it. All her efforts had been in vain. I heard this with satisfaction. Against the Ochrana, and therefore, to a certain extent, against me, not even an archduke could do anything, not even a Jewish lawyer. But in old Russia, as you know, there were three infallible means of getting what one wanted—and these she told him: Money, money, and money.

The dressmaker was prepared to pay. He took his leave, put on his curious furs, and drove away.

On the first evening on which his exhibition of "creations" was to take place, he appeared, friendly, rotund and yet rectangular, beaming, and dressed in a tailcoat and a white waistcoat with wonderful little red buttons which looked like ladybirds. He came out from behind the wings and took up a position in front of his girls' dressing rooms. But he was quite incapable of bribing even the least of us! He clinked a handful of silver coins in his tail pocket, like a monk with his collecting bag; and in spite of his resplendence he looked less like a potential briber than an actual begger. Even the most venal among us could never have taken any money from the man. One thing was clear: he was more at home with archdukes than with spies.

He disappeared. We went into the dressing rooms.

I was trembling. You must believe me when I tell you that at that moment I knew fear, real fear, hollow-eyed fear, for the first time in my life. I was afraid of Lutetia, afraid of my desire to see her, afraid of my eager anticipation, afraid of the unknown, of nakedness, of hesitation, afraid of my own power. So I turned around. I turned my back on her while she undressed. And she laughed at me. While I so fearfully turned my back, she may well have sensed, with the infallible instinct of a woman, the terror and impotence of a man in love; she probably realized that I was the most harmless spy in the whole of Russia. But what am I talking about instinct! She knew well enough that it was my duty to keep a close watch on her, and she had seen how I had turned my back and thereby delivered myself into her hands. I was already lost! She had already seen through me! Ah, my friends, it were better for a man to deliver himself over to his bitterest enemy than to let a woman see that he is in love with her. An enemy destroys quickly! But a woman....You will soon see how slowly, how murderously slowly....

Well! There I stood, with my face to the door, watching the immobile white handle, as though I had been ordered to spy upon this harmless little object. It was, as I can remember clearly, an ordinary porcelain door handle. Not even a crack was to be seen on it. I stood thus for a long time. And all the while my beloved sang and whistled and twittered behind my back—and in front of the mirror, as I discovered later—as carefree as the tender airs she sang. Yet in her singing, her whistling, her twittering, was derision. Nothing but derision . . . !

Suddenly there came a knock on the door. I turned around immediately, and of course saw Lutetia. She was sitting in front of an oval gold-framed mirror, trying to powder her back with an immense powder puff. She was already dressed. She was wearing a black dress, cut at the back into a low triangle which was edged with strips of blood-red satin, and she was trying, with her right hand, to reach her back in order to powder it with that oversized puff. More even than her nakedness had confused me, was I dazzled by this almost hellish—I can find no other expression for it—by this almost hellish combination of colors. From that hour I have firmly believed that the colors of Hell, which I shall certainly one day see for myself, are black, white, and red; and round the walls of Hell, here and there, will be seen the triangular outline of a woman's back; and the powder puff, too.

But the telling of all this takes too long, for it only lasted a moment. Before Lutetia could call: Come in!—the door opened. And even before I looked around, I already had a presentiment as to who the newcomer was. You will guess it, my friends! Who was it?—It was my old friend, my very old friend, Jenö Lakatos!

"Good evening!" he said in Russian. Thereafter he carried on a long conversation with Lutetia in French. I understood little of what was said. He seemed not to have recognized me—or not to have wished to recognize me. Lutetia turned round and smiled at him. She said a few words and smiled again, half leaning over the back of her chair and still holding the powder puff in her hand. I could see her double, her living self and her reflection. Lakatos walked over to her; he still limped visibly. He was wearing a tailcoat and patent leather shoes, and in his buttonhole glowed a red flower of a species unknown to me. As for me, I might not have been there. I felt certain that neither for Lutetia nor for Lakatos was I existent. I would almost have doubted my own presence in the dressing room, had I not seen how Lakatos drew up his sleeve—his cuffs were slightly frayed—and how he took the powder puff out of Lutetia's hand with two pointed fingers. And when he set to work, he did not simply powder the girl's back, but started to outline a completely new back; with both hands he began describing inexplicable circles in the air, first bending down, and then standing on tiptoe, his whole body stretched taut, until finally, at last, he touched Lutetia's back with the puff. And he powdered her back exactly as one would whitewash a wall. It took a long time, and Lutetia smiled—I could see her smile in the oval mirror. At last Lakatos turned to me, and in a matter-of-fact way, as though he had already seen me and greeted me, said: "Well, my friend, are you here too?" And at the same time he put his hand into his trouser pocket. There came a clinking of gold and silver coins. I knew the sound well enough.

"So, we have to meet again," he went on. I answered nothing. Finally, after a long silence, he asked: "How much longer are you going to bother this lady?"

"I bother her against my will," I said. "I am on duty here."

He lifted both hands towards the ceiling and exclaimed: "Duty! He's on duty!" And then he turned again to Lutetia and said something softly in French.

He beckoned me over to the oval mirror, close beside Lutetia, and said: "Your colleagues have all gone. All the other ladies have been left undisturbed. Understand?"

"I am on duty," I replied.

"I bribed them all," said Lakatos. "All of them. How much do you want?"

"Nothing!"

"Twenty? Forty? Sixty?"

"No!"

"A hundred?"

"No!"

"That is the most I am empowered to offer."

"Go yourself!"

At that moment the warning bell rang. Lutetia left the room.

"You will regret it!" said Lakatos. He went out after Lutetia, and I remained behind, confused and embarrassed. There was a cloying odor of rouge, perfume, powder, and woman about the room. I had not smelled it before; or perhaps I had simply not noticed it; how could I tell? Suddenly this diversity of scents surrounded me like an insidious enemy, and it seemed as though they had been left behind, not by Lutetia, but by my friend Lakatos. It seemed as though, before his arrival, the perfume, the rouge, the powder, and the woman had had no perceptible odor, and that only in his presence had they awoken to life.

I left the dressing room. I looked down the corridor. I looked into one dressing room after another. Nowhere did I find my colleagues. They were obliterated, spirited away, swallowed up. Twenty, forty, sixty, or a hundred rubles had slipped into their pockets.

I stood behind the wings, between two firemen, and I could see, sideways on, a part of the distinguished audience which had collected there to welcome a ridiculous dressmaker from Paris and which stood in awe of his wretched girls, called by them "mannequins." So the world had come down to this—I thought to myself—that it admired and reverenced a dressmaker! And Lakatos? Where had he come from? What wind had blown him here? He made me afraid. I felt plainly that I was in his power; I had long ago forgotten him, and therefore he made me doubly afraid. That is, I had never really forgotten him; I had only banished him, pushed him out of my thoughts, out of my consciousness. And so I was afraid—but with no ordinary fear, my friends, such as one has for one's fellow men! Not until that hour, and from the peculiar nature of my fear, did I properly realize who Lakatos was. I knew it now, but it was as though I were afraid of my own knowledge and had at all costs to endeavour to hide this knowledge from myself. It was as though I had been condemned rather to fight against myself and guard myself against myself, than to fight against him and guard myself against him. To such an extent, my friends, is a man blinded when the great Tempter so desires it. Man is indeed mightily afraid of the Devil, but he trusts him far more than he trusts himself.

During the first interval I again took up my position in Lutetia's dressing room. I persuaded myself that it was no more than my sense of duty demanded. But in reality it was the result of a remarkable impulse, a mixture of jealousy, obstinacy, amorousness, curiosity—and Heaven knows what else. Once again Lakatos appeared, while Lutetia was changing, and while I, exactly as before, stood with my back to her and stared at the door. Although I was actually standing in his way, he seemed to take as little notice of me as if I had been a wardrobe and not a human being at all. With a single elegant swing of his shoulders and hips, he evaded me. Already he stood behind Lutetia, so that she would see him in the mirror before which she had just sat down. His entry enraged me to such an extent that I even overcame my shame and forgot my love and promptly turned round. I was just in time to see Lakatos lay three fingers against his lips and blow a kiss to the reflection in the mirror. All the while he kept repeating incessantly the same French phrase: *Oh, mon amour, mon amour, mon amour!* Lutetia's reflection smiled. The next moment— I could not conceive then how he did it, and I still do not know today—Lakatos laid a huge bouquet of dark red roses on the table in front of the mirror. And I had seen him come into the room with his hands empty! Lutetia's reflection nodded lightly. Lakatos blew another kiss to her, turned round, and with the same circular motion by which he had eluded me on his entry, slipped past me and out of the room.

·   ·   ·

After I had seen with my own eyes that a bouquet of roses could suddenly be conjured out of nothingness, my professional alarm, so to speak, came to join my private fear. Like a pair of inseparable twins, they crouched within my breast. If a man could waft a bunch of roses out of thin air, then Lutetia, or even Lakatos, might easily produce with bare hands one of those bombs of which my superiors and their employers were so afraid. You must understand me: I was not worrying about the life of the Czar or the grand-dukes or the governors. What were the great men of this world to me, and why should I have bothered about them during those days? No, I trembled simply at the thought of the catastrophe, of the naked catastrophe, although I did not as yet know under what guise or in what form it would suddenly appear. But it seemed to me inevitable. And inevitable it seemed to me, also, that Lakatos should be its originator, *must* be its originator. I was never very religious by nature, and I had never trubled myself much with God and Heaven. But now I began to have a foretaste of Hell—and, just as one only calls the fire brigade after the fire has started, so I began during those days to offer up senseless, incoherent, but nevertheless desperately heartfelt and ardent prayers to the unknown Ruler of the world. They helped me little, evidently because I had not as then been tried sufficiently. Little did I suspect what lay in store for me.

I began to redouble my vigilance. The dressmaker was supposed to be staying only ten days in Russia, but already, after the third day, it was announced that his "creations" had so pleased our society ladies that it was proposed to prolong his visit by another ten days. What a wonderful and yet what a disturbing possibility! I was given orders to watch the well-known house of Madame Lukatchevski, where the officers of the garrison often used to gather after midnight. I knew it well, professionally, but only from the outside. Its interior I had not yet explored. I was given a so-called "expenses-allowance" of three hundred rubles and a "service" suit of tails, such as was usually shared between every three of our people in the higher division. Round my neck I hung a Greek order, a gold medal on the end of a red silk ribbon. Two of the lackeys at Madame Lukatchevski's were in our pay. At midnight I posted myself in front of the house. After having waited until such a time as I thought my presence would attract no attention, I went in, complete with top hat, cane, opera cloak, and orders. Those of the gentlemen, in uniform and civilian dress, about whom I had precise information, I greeted as if I were an old acquaintance. They smiled back at me with the disagreeable, empty smile with which one acknowledges friend and foe and neutral in the world of the great. Some time later one of our lackeys gave me a sign to follow him. He led me up to one of those discreet rooms on the first floor, whose presence was kept a secret from the ordinary habitués of the house. Such rooms were not for love—or what passed for love; on the contrary, they were reserved for witnesses and listeners, for informers and spies. Though a slit in the thin intervening partition one could hear and see everything that went on in the next room.

And I saw, my friends—I saw Lutetia, my beloved, together with young Prince Krapotkin. Oh, I recognized him immediately, there was no possible doubt. How could I *not* have recognized him! At that time I was so depraved that I could recognize something horrible more quickly than something pleasant and beautiful. Yes, I even practiced this quality and tried to perfect myself in it. So I saw Lutetia, my beloved, in the arms of the man whom I had once regarded as my archenemy; in the arms of the man whom I had almost forgotten during my last shameful years; in the arms of my hated false stepbrother, Prince Krapotkin.

.   .   .

You may perhaps realize, my friends, what took place inside me at that moment. Suddenly—for I had long since ceased to think of it—I was reminded of my ridiculous name, "Golubchik"; suddenly I remembered that I had only the Krapotkin family to thank for my present degrading profession; suddenly I believed that the old Prince would gladly have accepted me on that summer's day in Odessa had not the young boy burst into the room with such insolent cheerfulness; suddenly the mad vanity of my youth was reawakened—and all the bitterness. Yes, the bitterness, too! He—he was not the son of Krapotkin. I was! *I!* The name had only come to him by chance, and all that the name carried with it: the repute, the money, the world, and the first woman I had ever loved.

You know what that means, my friends: the first woman a man loves. She meant everything to me. I was a miserable creature, who might one day have become a decent man.

Now I would never become a decent man. In that moment when I saw Krapotkin and Lutetia together, the evil in me flared up, that evil which had been within me since my birth. Till then it had only flickered gently inside me, but now it roared up in a great open blaze. My fate was sealed.

I realized my fate even then, and because of that I was able to observe closely the two objects of my emotions; that of my hate and that of my love. Never does a man see so clearly and coolly as in the hour when he feels the black precipice before his feet. In that hour I felt that the love and the hatred in my heart were as inwardly united as the pair in the next room: Lutetia and Krapotkin. Just as little as the two I was watching, were my two feelings at variance; rather they were united into an overwhelming satisfaction, which was certainly greater and stronger and more sensual than the physical union of the pair.

I felt no desire, not even jealousy; at least not the common jealousy which each of us has probably felt when he has had to watch a beloved person being snatched away from him—or rather, when he has had to see the joy with which that person lets himself be snatched away. I was not even embittered. I had not even a desire for vengeance. Rather I was like a cold and objective judge who watches the exploits of the criminals whom he will later have to judge. I pronounced judgment then. It was death. Death for Krapotkin! I only marveled that I had waited so long. Yes, I realized then that this sentence of death had long lain inside me, pronounced, recorded, and sealed. It was, I repeat, no desire for revenge that prompted me to this. It was, in my opinion, the natural consequence of ordinary, objective, normal justice. Not I alone had fallen a victim to Krapotkin. No! The effective law of common justice was also his victim. And in the name of the law I pronounced judgment. It was death.

·   ·   ·

There lived in Petersburg at that time a certain police informer by the name of Leibusch. He was a tiny little man, scarcely four foot in height, not even a dwarf, but the shadow of a dwarf. He was a highly valued ally of those in our profession. I myself had only seen him once or twice, and then only for a few seconds. But to tell the truth, although I had, as they say, been washed by many waters, I was more than a little afraid of him. There were many unscrupulous blackguards and traitors in our company, but none smarter or more unscrupulous than he. For example, at a moment's notice he could produce proof that a confirmed criminal was as innocent as a lamb and that an innocent man had prepared a plot to assassinate the Czar. But I, although I had already sunk so low, still cherished the conviction that I did not do evil from innate wickedness but because fate had condemned me to it. Incredible as it may seem, I still considered myself a "good man." I at least was still conscious that I acted evilly and that I must therefore justify myself to myself. Vileness had been forced upon me. My name was Golubchik. Every right which I had, from my birth onwards, had been taken away from me. At that time, my misfortune seemed, in my eyes, a totally undeserved disaster. To a certain extent, therefore, I had a fully documented right to be evil. But the others, who practiced evil upon me, had certainly no such right.

Well, I sought out our informer, Leibusch. In the first moment, when I stood before him, I was suddenly conscious of the terrible thing I was proposing to do. His yellowish skin, his red-rimmed eyes, his great pock-marks, his tiny inhuman figure almost shook my firm belief that I was a judge and an instrument of justice. Several times I hesitated before bringing myself to broach the purpose of my visit.

"Leibusch," I said, "here is a chance for you to prove your ability." We were in the anteroom of our chief, sitting side by side on a bright green plush sofa, and it seemed to me as though it were already the dock; yes, I was sitting in the dock at the very hour when I had taken it upon myself to judge and to condemn.

"What more do you want me to prove?" said the little man. "I've proved enough already!"

"I need," I said, "material against a certain person."

"Someone important?"

"Of course."

"Who is it?"

"The young Krapotkin."

"Not difficult," said the little man. "Not at all difficult!"

How easy it was! The little man was in no way astonished that I needed material against Krapotkin. So they had long been collecting material against him! I almost thought myself magnanimous for not having known that before. What I intended was hardly a base piece of treachery, it was almost an honorable duty.

"When?" I asked.

"Tomorrow, at the same time," said the little man.

He possessed really wonderful material. The half of what he brought would have been sufficient to condemn an ordinary Russian to twenty years in Siberia. We sat in the quiet back room of a restaurant whose owner I knew, and examined the material. It consisted of letters to friends, officers and highly placed personages, to well known anarchists and suspect writers, and a number of extremely convincing photographs. "This one," said the little man, "and this one and this one, I forged."

I stared at him. His little face, in which there was scarcely space for his eyes, nose, and mouth, and whose thin cheeks were sunken and hollow, was emotionless. In that face the features had no room to alter their expression. He said: "I forged that." And: "I forged that." And: "I forged that." And not a flicker or change in his expression. It was plainly a matter of indifference to him whether the pictures were real or forged. They were just pictures. More than pictures—they were proof. And since he had learned in the course of many years that forged pictures could prove just as much as genuine ones, he had completely forgotten how to distinguish between the two; and with almost childish simplicity he believed that the forgeries, which he himself had made, were no forgeries at all. Yes. I believe that he no longer knew what was the difference between a forged photograph and a real one, or how a real letter differed from one of his own forgeries. It would have been wrong to have regarded this Leibusch, this tiny man, as a criminal. He was a lost soul, far worse than a criminal, fouler even than I, my friends

I knew exactly what I had to do with the letters and the pictures. My hatred had a purpose. But this little man was no hater and no judge. Everything that he did was purposeless; the Devil simply commanded him. He was as stupid as an ox, but brilliantly clever in doing difficult things whose sense and purpose he could not understand. He never even demanded a small earthly reward. He did it all to oblige others. He asked me for no money, no promise, no pledge. He handed over to me the whole of that valuable material, without a change of expression, without asking why I needed it, without demanding anything in return—without even knowing who I was. He had received his reward elsewhere, so it seemed.

Well, what had that got to do with me? I took what I needed; I did not ask where it came from, nor from whom. I simply took it from the little man.

Less than half an hour later I was in the presence of my immediate superior. And two hours later young Krapotkin was arrested

•   •   •

He did not remain long under arrest, my friends, not at all long. Three days in all. On the third I was summoned by our chief and he spoke to me as follows:

"Young man, I thought you were cleverer than that."

I said nothing.

"Young man," he began again, "explain your extremely stupid action to me."

"Highness," I said, "I have probably been stupid—because you yourself say so. But I cannot explain my action."

"Very well," he replied—"then I shall explain it to you. You are in love. And I am going to take this opportunity to make a few philosophical remarks. Pay attention to what I have to say. A man who wishes to make something of his life is never in love. But, more especially, a man who has the good fortune to work for us has no feelings whatsoever. He may desire a certain woman—good, I can understand that. But when someone greater stands in his way, he must repress his desire. Listen to me, young man. All my life I have only had one desire: to become great and powerful. I have succeeded; today I am both. I watch over His Majesty himself, our Czar—God grant him health and happiness. And why am I in a position to do that? Because never in my long life have I loved or hated anyone. I renounced every pleasure—and for that reason I have never known real suffering. I was never in love; so I know no jealousy. I never hated; so I have no desire for revenge. I have never spoken the truth;

so I have never known the satisfaction that comes from a successful lie. Young man, model yourself on me!—I must punish you. The Prince is powerful, he will never forget the affront. For the sake of a ridiculous little girl you have ruined your career. And for me, too, you have earned a severe and unpleasant reprimand. I have considered carefully what punishment you deserve. And I have decided to inflict on you the severest of all punishments. You are hereby condemned to follow this ridiculous woman. I condemn you, in a manner of speaking, to eternal love. You will go to Paris as our agent. On the day you arrive, you will go to our Embassy and report to S. Here are your papers. God be with you, young man. That is the hardest judgment I have ever pronounced in my life."

At that time I was young, my friends, and I was in love. After His Highness had passed judgment, something extraordinary happened to me, something ridiculous. I felt an unknown power forcing me to my knees. I actually fell on my knees before our chief and I fumbled for his hand to kiss it. He drew it sharply away from me and ordered me to get to my feet and cease such foolishness. Ah! He was great and powerful—because he was inhuman. Of course, he understood nothing of what was going on inside me. He threw me out.

Outside in the corridor, I looked at my papers. And I grew rigid with happiness and amazement. My papers were made out in the name of Krapotkin. My passport was

made out in that name. In a covering letter to the Embassy
in Paris I was expressly described as an agent whose duty
it was to watch over the so-called subversive Russian ele-
ment in France. What a hideous task, my friends! And yet
at the time it seemed fine to me. How depraved I was then!
Depraved and lost. All depraved people are really those
who have lost their way.

Two days later the dressmaker, together with his girls,
left Petersburg. Shortly before his departure he was introduced to me. In his stupid and vain eyes I was a representative of the nobility of Russia, a prince and at the
same time a Krapotkin—for he may really have imagined
that he had been given a genuine prince as an escort. And
I too, having for the first time a passport in the name of
Krapotkin in my pocket, persuaded myself that this was
so. But all the while I felt in the depths of my heart the
two-fold, the three-fold insult which had been paid to
me. For I *was* a Krapotkin, a Krapotkin by blood; and I
was a spy; and I bore the name which was mine by right
only by virtue of my position in the police. In a most
wrongful way I had bought and stolen what should have
come to me by right. So I thought at the time, my
friends, and I would probably have been extremely
unhappy had it not been for my love for Lutetia. But
that—my love I mean—excused and obliterated everything. I was with Lutetia, at her side. I was accompanying
her. I stayed in the town where she was staying. I desired
her. I wanted her with all my senses. I burned for her, as

one says. But for the first I took no notice of her. I tried to appear indifferent; and of course I hoped that she would notice me of her own accord and would let me know by a glance, an expression, a smile, that *she* had noticed me. But she did nothing. Most certainly she had not noticed me. And why should she?

That was, indeed, during the first twelve hours of our journey. And why should she have noticed me in the first twelve hours?

We had to make a detour. We did not travel direct to Paris; for the society ladies who happened to be in Moscow at that time, or who lived there permanently, were unwilling to let the famous dressmaker leave Russia without at least having seen him and his dolls. So they demanded that we should stay a day in Moscow. Good! We would stop a day in Moscow. We arrived early one afternoon and drove to the Hotel Europe. For each of the girls I ordered a bouquet of dark red roses, all the same. But only in the bouquet destined for Lutetia did I insert my visiting card. Oh, of course, not my real one. I had never had such a thing in my life. But I now had no less than five hundred cards, false ones, in the name of Krapotkin.

I must admit that I often pulled one out of my pocket-book and gazed at it. I feasted my eyes on it. The longer I looked at it, the more I began to believe in its genuineness. I saw myself in this false visiting card, somewhat as a woman sees herself in a mirror which makes her appear

more charming than she is. And as though I did not know
that my passport was a false one, I would sometimes take
it out and reassure myself by its official statement that my
visiting card had not lied.

So stupid and vain was I at that time, my friends,
although a far greater force held me in thrall. But even that
force, namely my love, fed itself on my vanity and my
stupidity.

•   •   •

We finally stayed two days in Moscow, and the society
ladies came from near and far. On both afternoons in the
hotel, there was a short and, so to speak, condensed display. The fashionable dressmaker did not trouble to put
on his tail suit. He wore a violet morning coat, a pale
pink silk shirt, and a pair of brown patent leather shoes.
The ladies were enchanted by him. He welcomed them
all in a long speech. And they replied by chanting his
praises at still greater length. Although at that time
my knowledge of French was still negligible, I noticed
that the ladies were at pains to imitate the dressmaker's
pronunciation. I myself avoided speaking with them,
because one or the other would most likely have recognized that I was not a Krapotkin—if only from my lam-
entable French. But I was safe enough, for they only took
notice of the dressmaker and his "creations." Mostly of
the dressmaker! And how gladly, in spite of all their

femininity, would they have worn a violet morning suit
and a pale pink silk shirt!

But enough of these fruitless reflections. Every age has
its ridiculous dressmakers, its ridiculous fashions, its ridiculous women. The women who today in Russia wear the
uniform of the Red Front are the daughters of those same
women who had once been prepared to put on a violet
morning coat; and the daughters of the Red Front today
will some time perhaps wear similar clothes to those of
their grandmothers.

We left Moscow. We arrived at the frontier. At the very
moment in which the train drew up, there came to me for
the first time the sudden realisation that I was in danger of
losing Lutetia if I did not do something quickly. But what
to do? What does a lost man of my type do, a man who
practices the most despicable of all trades? Ah, my friends,
he never has the direct, inspired, godlike imagination of
those who are simply in love. A man of my cast has a base,
distorted imagination. He pursues the woman he loves
with every means offered him by his profession. Not even
his feelings can ennoble a man of my type. To misuse power
is the guiding principle of men like me! And God knows,
I misused it.

At the frontier I gave one of my colleagues a sign, and
he understood it immediately. You will remember, my
friends, what the Russian frontier meant in those days.
It was less the boundary of the all-powerful empire of
the Czar than the bounds of our despotism; that is, of the

despotism of the Russian police. The might of the Czar had its limits, even in his own palace. But our might, the might of the police, only ceased at the frontiers of the empire, and often—as you will soon hear—far beyond the frontiers. Nevertheless it gave a police official inexpressible pleasure, firstly to see a harmless person tremble with fear, secondly to do a favor for a colleague, and thirdly—and this is particularly important—to frighten a pretty young woman. That, my friends, is the peculiar expression of police eroticism.

My colleague immediately understood me. I disappeared for a time and waited in the police bureau. The dressmaker and all his girls were subjected to a most distressing and thorough search—and nothing could avert it, neither his persuasive tongue nor his appeals in the name of all the nobility of Russia. The officials simply did not understand French. In vain he called for me, for Prince Krapotkin. I could, indeed, observe him through the little window set in the wall between the police bureau and the customs room. But he did not see me. I remained invisible. I saw how he fussed round amongst his terrified troupe of girls, important and helpless, self-confident and lost, simultaneously pompous and afraid, as arrogant as a cock, as timid as a hare, as stupid as a donkey. I enjoyed the sight. I admit it. I should really have had no time to watch and despise him. For I was in love with Lutetia. But such was my nature, my friends! Often, indeed, I do not know what to think of myself. . . .

But that is not the most important thing. The chief thing was that suddenly, thanks to the friendly disposition of my colleague, a revolver was discovered in Lutetia's trunk. The dressmaker ran helplessly around. Several times he called for me, he invoked my name, as one invokes the names of one's gods—but still I refused to show myself. From my spy hole I peeped out, evil and contented, a god and a spy, and I saw Lutetia, pale, desperate. She did what all women have to do in such situations: she began to cry. And I remembered that I had watched her through a similar spy hole, scarcely two weeks before, and that I had seen her in the arms of the young Krapotkin, happy and laughing. Oh, I had not forgotten the sound of that laugh. And so vile was I, my friends, that I had an intense feeling of satisfaction. Let the train wait, two hours, three hours! I had time enough.

At last, when matters had got so far that Lutetia, bereft of words, had fallen upon the dressmaker's neck, and all the other girls had begun to flutter round so that the whole scene looked like a cross between a tragic massacre, an excited chicken yard, and the romantic adventure of a romantic dressmaker—I appeared on the scent. Immediately my colleague bowed before me and said: "Your Highness, at your service!"

I took no notice of him. I called into the room, without looking at any of the numerous people there: "What is the matter here?"

"Your Highness," began my colleague, "a revolver has been found in a lady's trunk."

"That is my revolver," I said. "The ladies are under my protection."

"At your command, Highness," said the official.

We returned to the train.

•   •   •

Of course—as I expected—scarcely had we got into the train than the dressmaker began pouring out his gratitude. "Who is that lady with the revolver," I asked. "A harmless girl," he said. "I cannot understand it." "I would like to speak to her," I said. "Immediately," he replied. "I will bring her to you."

He brought her to me. And he left us forthwith. We were alone, Lutetia and I.

It was already growing dark, and the train seemed to race ever faster through the gathering twilight. It seemed extraordinary to me that she did not recognize me. It was as though everything were in league to prove to me how little time I had to reach my goal. Therefore it seemed to me advisable to say at once: "Where is my revolver now?"

Instead of an answer—which would still have been possible—Lutetia fell into my arms.

I took her on to my lap. And in the twilight of the evening, which came in through the two windows on each side of us—it was no longer one evening, but two—there began those caresses which you all know, and which so often prelude the tragedy of our lives."

·   ·   ·

When he had reached this stage in his story, Golubchik fell silent for a long while. His silence appeared to us even longer than it was, because he drank nothing. We, too, only sipped at our glasses, out of shame and reserve, because Golubchik scarcely seemed to notice his glass. His silence therefore seemed in a way a double silence. A storyteller who breaks his narrative and does not raise to his lips the glass which stands before him, arouses an extraordinary feeling of uneasiness in his hearers. We all of us, Golubchik's audience, felt uneasy. We were ashamed of looking Golubchik in the face; we stared almost stupidly at our glasses. If only we could have heard the ticking of a clock. But no. Not even a clock ticked, not a fly buzzed, and from the dark streets outside not a sound came through the thick iron shutters. We were at the mercy of the deathly silence. Long, long eternities seemed to have passed since the moment when Golubchik had begun his story. Eternities, I say, not hours. For since the clock on the wall had stopped, and since each of us threw a stealthy glance at it, although we all knew that it had stopped, it seemed as though Time had ceased; and the hands on the white face were no longer simply black, but frankly ominous. Yes, they were as ominous as eternity. They were

unchanging in their obstinate, almost treacherous, immo-
bility, and it seemed to us as though they stood still, not
because the dock work had stopped, but from a sort of
malice and as if to prove that the story which Golubchik
was telling us was an eternally recurring, eternally hopeless
story, independent of time and space, of day and night. And
since time stood still, the room too, in which we were sitting, became exempt from all laws of space; and it was as
though we were no longer on solid earth, but floating on
the eternal waters of the eternal sea. It seemed as though
we were in a ship. And our sea was the night.

·   ·   ·

Now at last, after that long pause, Golubchik took a
gulp from his glass.

"I have considered"—he began again—"whether I
should relate to you my subsequent experiences on the
train. But I would rather omit that. I will therefore begin
immediately with my arrival in Paris.

So I arrived in Paris. I need not tell you what Paris
meant to me, to Golubchik, the spy who despised himself,
to the false Krapotkin, the lover of Lutetia. It cost me an
immense effort *not* to believe that my passport was false
and to forget that my vile task of watching refugees, who
were a so-called "menace to the State," was my own. But it
cost me unbelievable agony at last to persuade myself that

my existence was a living lie, my name a borrowed one, if
not stolen, and my passport the infamous document of an
infamous spy. And from the moment when I recognized all
that, I began to hate myself. I had always hated myself, my
friends! After all that I have told you, you will have realized
that. But the hatred which I now felt for myself was hatred
of a different kind. For the first time I felt contempt for
myself. Previously I had never realized that a false existence, founded on a borrowed and stolen name, could
destroy one's own, one's real existence. But now I learned
in my own person the inexplicable magic of a word; of a
written, an inscribed word. Of course a stupid, thoughtless
police official had made me out a passport in the name of
Krapotkin; and he had not only not thought anything
about it, but had taken it as a matter of course that a spy
called Golubchik should be lent the name of Krapotkin.
Nevertheless, it was magic. There is magic in every spoken,
let alone every written, word. Through the simple fact of
possessing a passport made out in the name of Krapotkin,
I *was* Krapotkin; but at the same time this passport proved
to me, in a different, quite irrational way, that I had
obtained it not only unrighteously but also for dishonest
purposes. To a certain extent it was a constant witness
of my evil conscience. It compelled me to become a
Krapotkin, while, all the times I could never cease to be
a Golubchik. I was a Golubchik, I am a Golubchik, and a
Golubchik I will remain, my friends . . . ! But moreover
—and that "moreover" is significant and important—

I was in love with Lutetia. And she, who had given herself to me, was perhaps—who can tell?—in love with that Prince Krapotkin whom I was impersonating. To myself, therefore, I was to a certain extent Golubchik, even if with the firm belief that I was a Krapotkin; but to her who at that time had to imagine my past life, I was a Krapotkin, a cousin of the young lieutenant of the Guards, my half-brother, whom I hated and who had embraced her before me.

I say: before me. For at the age at which I then was, it is usual for a young man to hate with a deep hatred all those men who have, as they say, "possessed" his beloved before him. But why should I not hate my false half-brother? My father, my name, and the woman I loved, he had taken from me! If I could call any man my enemy, he was that man. I had not yet forgotten how he had burst into the room of my father—not his father—in order to drive me out. I hated him. Ah, how I hated him! Who, if not he, was responsible for my entering the foulest of all professions? Again and again he crossed my path. I was powerless against him; he was omnipotent against me. Yes, again and again he stood in my way to thwart me. Not Prince Krapotkin had begot him. Another had done that. And already in the moment when that other had begot him, he had begun to defraud me. Oh, I hated him, my friends! How I hated him!

But spare me the closer details of how I became Lutetia's lover. It was not difficult. It was not easy. I was in love, my friends, and even today I find it hard to say whether it was difficult or easy for me to become Lutetia's lover. It was difficult and easy, it was easy and difficult—whichever you prefer . . . !

·   ·   ·

In those days I had no very exact ideas of the world and of the curious laws which govern love. I was, indeed, a spy, and therefore, one would think, a jack-of-all-trades. But in spite of my profession and in spite of all the experiences which it had brought me, I was a harmless fool with regard to Lutetia; with regard to Lutetia—that is, to all women; with regard to the whole of womankind. For Lutetia was woman, plain and simple—she was womankind personified. She was the woman of my life. She was the woman, the feminine in my life.

Today, my friends, it is easy to deride the situation in which I then found myself. Today I am old and experienced. Today we are all old and experienced. But each of you will be able to remember an hour when you were young and foolish. With you, perhaps, it was only an hour, measured by the clock. But with me it was a long hour, far too long an hour . . . as you will soon see.

·   ·   ·

As I had been ordered, and as was my duty, I reported at the Russian Embassy.

There was a man there, a man, I tell you, who attracted me at the first glance. He even attracted me strongly. He was a huge, powerful man. He was a handsome, powerful man. He should rather have been in the Imperial Guard than in our Secret Police. Till then I had never seen a man of his type in our company. Yes, I must admit that after I had spoken to him for scarcely a quarter of an hour it almost pained me to know that he was in a position in which he could never escape from vileness and treachery. Yes, it actually pained me. So strongly did he radiate a genuine, inward peace. How shall I describe it: it was a harmonious power, the characteristic of real kindliness. "I have heard about you," he greeted me. "I know what foolishness you have been up to. Well now, under which name do you propose to live here?"

Under which name? Well, I had one, the only one which fitted me. My name was Krapotkin. I had visiting-cards. Such were my wretched reflections at the time. For the past few years I had practiced every sort of deceit—and nothing, one might think, could make a man more astute, more experienced, more discerning, than spying. But no; one would be wrong. My victims were not only finer men than I, but also considerably cleverer; and the simplest among them would have found it impossible to be as vain and ridiculous and childish as I was. I was already in the depths of Hell. Yes, I was already a hardened servitor of Hell, and still—I felt it at that moment—the one, stupid, blind, driving-force of my life was my chagrin at the name

of Golubchik and at the degradation to which I considered
I had been subjected, and my mania to become a
Krapotkin at any price. I still believed that through cun-
ning and treachery I could wipe out what I deemed to be
the stigma in my life. But I only heaped disgrace after disgrace upon my own miserable head. At that moment, too,
I felt vaguely that I had never really followed Lutetia out
of love for her, and that I had merely imagined a great passion, such as only noble souls can experience, for my own
justification. In reality, I had simply made up my mind to
possess her, just as I had made up my mind no longer to be
a Golubchik. Within myself, and therefore against myself I
had evolved one mad folly after another. I had deceived
and betrayed myself, exactly as I was supposed to be
deceiving and betraying others. I had woven myself into
my own net. It was too late. Although I realized all this, half
clearly, half unclearly, I still compelled myself to cling to the
lie that everything was because of Lutetia, and that for her
sake alone I could not surrender my false name of
Krapotkin. "I have already a name," I said, and showed him
my passport. He ignored it and said: "My young friend, to
work here with that name you must indeed be clever. You
know that you have been allotted the definite duties of an
intermediary agent. But you may have private reasons for
your choice. There is probably a woman somewhere
about. Let us hope that she is young and pretty. I will only
remind you that young and pretty women need money.
And I am very economical. I only pay unusual premiums

for unusual services. I shall make no exception in your
case. False papers, in other names, you can have as many as
you want. You may go now. Report to me as often as you
wish. Where are you staying? In the Hotel Louvois, I know
it. One thing more. Learn languages, take lessons, go to the
High School if you like. You will report to me at least twice
a week, here, during the evening. Here is a check. That you
will be watched by your colleagues, you know already. So
no foolishness!"

When I got outside I breathed deeply. I felt that I had
been through one of those hours which, when one is
young, one calls decisive. Later in life, one comes to recognize that many, in fact most hours are decisive. Admittedly
there are crises and climaxes and so-called peripetiae, but
we ourselves know nothing of them, and it is quite impossible for us to distinguish between a moment of climax and
any ordinary moment. At the most, we experience this and
that—and even then the experience is of no use to us. But
the power to recognize and to distinguish is denied us.

Our imagination is always stronger than our conscience. Although my conscience told me that I was a
scoundrel, a weakling, a wretch, I was unable to accept the
miserable truth, for my imagination rode away with me at
a terrible gallop. With a comfortable check in my pocket,
temporarily dismissed by my chief, whom indeed I now
thought as intolerable as he had previously seemed kindly,
I felt free and unbounded in a free and unbounded Paris.
Adventures, glorious adventures, lay on every side, and I

was on my way to meet the most beautiful woman in the world and the most fashionable of all dressmakers. In that hour it seemed to me that I was at last beginning the sort of life which I had always longed for. Now I was almost a real Krapotkin. And I suppressed the importunate but almost inaudible voice of conscience which insisted that I was really on my way towards a twofold, even a threefold, captivity: firstly the captivity of my foolishness, my indiscretion, my depravity, to all of which, however, I was already accustomed; secondly to the captivity of my love; and thirdly to the captivity of my profession.

• • •

It was a mild, sunny, Parisian, winter's afternoon. The good people were sitting on the terraces outside the cafés, and with blissful contentment I thought how, at the same time of day and year in Russia, the good people would be huddled together in hot, dark rooms. I wandered aimlessly from one café to another. Everywhere the people, the shopkeepers, the waiters seemed to be happy and benevolent, blessed with that benevolence which only a lasting happiness can give. Winter in Paris was a real spring. The women in Paris were real women. The men in Paris were cordial companions. The waiters in Paris were like happy, alert white-aproned minions of some bountiful god from the Golden Age. And in Russia, which I believed I had left for ever, it was dark and cold. It was as though I were no

longer in the terrible service of that country. There lived
the Golubchiks, whose miserable name I only bore because
I had happened to come into the world in my father's
house. There lived the no less miserable Krapotkins, miserable in character, a princely race such as could only be
found in Russia, a race which denied its own flesh and
blood. Never would a French Krapotkin have behaved like
that. I was, as you can see, young, stupid, miserable, and
pitiable. But to myself I appeared proud, noble and victorious. Everything that I saw in this wonderful city seemed
to confirm my convictions, my previous actions, and my
love for Lutetia.

Only when evening came—far too early for my lik-
ing—hurried on by the artificial efforts of the street lamps,
did my mood change. A feeling of despondency came over
me, and I appeared to myself like some disappointed
believer who has lost his gods. I hailed a *fiacre* and drove to
my hotel. And with all my strength I clung to the one hope
that was left me, to Lutetia. To Lutetia and to tomorrow.
Tomorrow I would see her. Tomorrow, tomorrow!

I began to do what our type always does in such circumstances: I began to drink. First beer, then wine, then
schnapps. In time the heaviness began to lift from my
heart, and by the early hours of the morning I had almost
attained the same feeling of blissfulness as that which had
filled me in the afternoon.

When I went out into the streets, no longer quite sure
of my movements, the mild winter's morning was already

graying in the sky. It was raining, softly and kindly, as it can only rain in April in Russia. That and my mental confusion made me forget for a moment the time and place of my present being. I was astonished and almost frightened when I saw the servility with which the employees of the hotel treated me. I had first to remind myself that I was actually Prince Krapotkin.

The memory of it returned to me after a time, outside in the soft fresh morning rain. It was as though the rain itself had baptized me Prince Krapotkin. A Parisian Prince Krapotkin. And that, in my opinion, meant far more than a Russian one.

It rained out of the Parisian sky, softly and kindly, upon my bare head, upon my tired shoulders. I stood for a long time in front of the hotel steps. Behind my back I could feel the respectful, the elaborately indifferent, glances of the staff. And, thanks to my professional instinct, I could also feel something of mistrust in those glances. But they did me good. The rain did me good. The sky above blessed me. Morning in Paris was already beginning. Newspaper sellers moved past with curiously brisk indifference. The people of Paris were waking. And I, as though I were not a Golubchik but a real Krapotkin, a Parisian Krapotkin, yawned, with weariness indeed, but no less with arrogance. And arrogantly, leisurely, with the perfect air of a *grand seigneur,* I walked past the respectful, mistrustful glances of the hotel staff, whose backs were bent for a Krapotkin and whose eyes seemed to stare at the spy Golubchik.

Confused and exhausted I sank into my bed. On the windowsill outside the rain pattered monotonously.

•   •   •

I now entered upon, as I had decided—or, if you like, as I had imagined—a new existence. With new clothes— for I had summoned one of those ridiculous tailors who at that time used to dress the so-called gentlemen of fashion—I began to lead the sort of life which seemed to me suited to a prince. A truly new sort of life. Several times I was invited by my beloved Lutetia's dressmaker. Several times I invited him to my hotel. Since my old shame is so far fallen from me that I can tell you my story as openly as I am now doing, you will believe me, my friends, when I assure you that it is not out of pride or conceit when I say that at that time I was gifted with a great talent for languages. Within a week I could speak almost perfect French. At all events, I could converse fluently with the fashionable dressmaker and his girls, who all knew me from the journey. I also conversed with Lutetia. Of course she remembered me, especially from the incident at the frontier, and also because of my name, and finally on account of the hour she had spent in my compartment. At that time I was nothing more than the bearer of my false name. I had long since ceased to be myself. I was not only not a Krapotkin, I was also not a Golubchik. I was as though between Heaven and earth. More still: between Heaven and earth and Hell. In none of those three worlds did I feel at home. Where was I really? And what was I really? Was I Golubchik? Was I Krapotkin? Was I in love with Lutetia? Was I in love with her or with my new existence? Was it even a new existence? Was I lying or was I telling the truth? At that time I sometimes thought of my poor mother, the wife of the forester Golubchik. She knew of me no more; I had vanished from the narrow circle of faces before her poor old eyes. No longer had I even a mother left. A mother! What other person in the whole, wide world was without a mother? I was lost and desolate. But such a wretch was I then, that I even extracted a certain pride from my misery; and, since I myself had brought it about, I regarded it as a sort of distinction which fate had conferred upon me.

But I will try to be brief. After a few entirely unnecessary visits to the great dressmaker, and after having seen and praised his new "creations," I succeeded in gaining with Lutetia that particular kind of intimacy which implies an engagement between two people. A short while afterwards I had the doubtful pleasure of being a guest in her house.

•　　•　　•

In her house! What I call "house" was a miserable hotel in the rue de Montmartre. It was a tiny room. The browny-yellow wallpaper depicted an endless repetition of two parrots, a chrome yellow one and a snow white one, perpetually kissing one another. They were caressing. Those parrots had all the qualities of doves. Yes, even the wallpaper affected me deeply. It seemed to me unworthy of Lutetia that, just in her room, parrots had to behave like doves. And it had to be parrots. At that time I hated parrots. Today, I no longer know why. (Incidentally, I also hated doves.)

I brought flowers and caviar with me, the two gifts which I thought should characterize a Russian prince. We had long conversations together, deep and intimate. "You know my cousin?" I asked, innocently and mendaciously. "Yes, little Sergei," she answered, equally innocently and equally mendaciously. "He made love to me," she continued. "For hours on end! He sent me orchids. Think of it! Me, of all the girls! But I didn't take any notice of him. I didn't care for him."

"I don't care for him, either," I said. "I've known him ever since he was a boy, and even then I didn't care for him."

"You are right," said Lutetia. "He is a beast."

"But still," I began, "you had a rendezvous with him in Petersburg, and he himself told me that it was in a *chambre séparée* at old Lukatchevski's."

"He was lying, he was lying," screamed Lutetia, as only women can scream when they obviously wish to deny the truth. "I have never been with any man in a *chambre séparée*. Neither in Russia nor in France!"

"Don't shout so," I said, "and don't lie. I saw you myself. I saw you. You must have forgotten it. My cousin never lies."

As could not otherwise be expected, Lutetia began to sob brokenly. I, who cannot bear to see a woman crying, ran downstairs and ordered a bottle of cognac. When I returned, Lutetia was no longer crying. She only behaved as though the lie in which I had caught her had utterly exhausted her and drained her of all strength. "Don't worry!" I said. "I've brought you a restorative."

She got up after a while. "Don't let's talk any more about your cousin," she said.

"All right, we won't talk about him any more," I agreed. "Let us talk about you."

And she told me everything—all of which I strangely enough accepted as absolute truth, although I had heard her lie only a few minutes before. She was the daughter of a rag-and-bone merchant. Seduced at an early age, that is, at sixteen, which today I can no longer call "early," she ran away with a jockey who loved her and left her in a hotel in Rouen. Oh, she was never lacking in men! She did not remain long in Rouen. And because she was so strikingly beautiful, the fashionable dressmaker, who was then search-ing among the crowds of Paris for models, had noticed her. . . . And so she had come to work for the fashionable dressmaker. . . .

She had drunk too much. She was still lying, I realized that after the first half-hour. But where, my friends, can one find the truth which one would like to hear from the lips of the girl one loves? And had not I lied myself? Was not I living completely enmeshed in lies? And was I not so comfortably nested in falsehood that I not only enjoyed my own lies, but also recognized and treasured those of others? Of course, Lutetia was as little the daughter of a rag-and-bone merchant or a concierge or a shoemaker or anything else, as I was a prince. Had she then suspected who I really was, she would probably have persuaded me that she was the illegitimate daughter of a baron. But since she had to assume that I was at home among barons, and since she knew that high-born people regard the poor and lowly with an almost poetic melancholy and love the fairy story about the blessings of poverty, she too told me the fable about the wonders of being poor. Actually, while she spoke, she sounded quite credible. For years she had been living among lies, among those special lies, and at times she even believed in her own story. She was lost, just as I was lost. And a lost person lies as innocently as a child. A lost existence demands a foundation of lies. In reality, Lutetia was the daughter of a once fashionable dressmaker, and the man in whose employ she now was had not sought for his girls among the crowds of Paris, but, naturally enough, among the daughters of his colleagues.

But besides all that, my friends, Lutetia was beautiful. Beauty always appears credible. The Devil, who determines men's judgments on women, fights on the side of the beautiful and attractive. We seldom believe the truth from an ugly woman; but from a beautiful one we believe every word she utters.

It is difficult to say what it was about Lutetia that attracted me so greatly. At the very first glance she appeared different from all the other girls. Also she was made up and looked like a creature of wax and porcelain, a mixture of which mannequins were made at that time. Today, of course, the world has made great progress, and the women are made of different and ever-changing materials for each season of the year. Lutetia, too, had an unnaturally small mouth, and as long as she kept silent it looked like a narrow piece of coral. Her eyebrows, also, formed two unnaturally perfect arches, constructed almost according to geometrical rules; and when she lowered her eyes, one could see improbably long, artificially blackened eyelashes, curtains of eyelashes. The way she sat down, leaned back, the way she got up and the way she walked, the way she picked up a thing and put it down again, all these were, of course, practiced and the outcome of numerous rehearsals. Even her slender fingers seemed to have been in some way stretched and carved by a surgeon. They were slightly reminiscent of pencils. She played with her fingers while she spoke, watching them attentively, and it almost seemed as though she were searching for her reflection in her brightly polished nails. Only seldom was any expression to be found in her blue eyes. But when she spoke, and in the few moments when she forgot herself, her mouth became broad and almost lascivious, and between her gleaming teeth there appeared for a fraction of a second her moist tongue, alive, a red and venomous little animal. It was with her mouth that I had fallen in love, with her mouth. All the wickedness of women is to be found in their mouths. That is, by the way, the home of treachery and, as you all know from your Catechism, the birthplace of original sin. . . .

So I loved her. I was staggered by her mendacious story and just as staggered by the little hotel room and the parrot wallpaper. The surroundings in which she lived were unworthy of her, and more particularly unworthy of her mouth. I remembered the face of the hotelier, as he sat below in his box, looking like a sort of dog in shirt-sleeves—and I made up my mind to provide for Lutetia a happier, kindlier existence.

"Would you allow me," I asked, "to help you? Please don't misunderstand me. I make no demands. Helping people affords me great pleasure," I lied, because destruction was my profession. "I have nothing else to do. Unfortunately I have no profession. So would you allow me . . . ?"

"On what conditions?" asked Lutetia, sitting down on the bed.

"On no conditions, as I have already told you."

"All right !" she said. And since I made a move to get by she began: "Please don't think that I am unhappy here. But our lord and master, whom you know, is very often bad-tempered—and I have the misfortune to be more dependent on his temper than the other girls. You know" —and now her tongue began to distill poison—"they all have their rich and noble friends. But I, I prefer to be alone and respectable. I don't sell myself!" she added after a while and jumped up from the bed. Her dressing-gown, pink with blue flowers, gaped open. No! She didn't sell herself. She was only offering herself to me.

•　　•　　•

From now on began the most confused period of my life. I rented a little maisonette near the Champs Élysées, one of those houses which at that time used to be called "love nests." Lutetia herself arranged it according to her tastes. Again there were parrots on the walls—a genus of birds which, as I have already said, I loathed. There was a piano although Lutetia could not play, two cats, of whose noiseless and startling jumps I was greatly afraid, a fireplace without a draught, in which the fire immediately went out—and lastly, so to speak a special compliment to myself, a genuine Russian samovar made of brass, which I was chosen to operate. There was a pleasing parlor maid in a suitable and pleasing dress—she looked as though she had come from a special factory for parlor maids—and, as a crowning touch, which enraged me beyond bounds, there was a genuine live parrot which learned, with uncanny quickness and almost malicious genius, to repeat my false name "Krapotkin," thus continually reminding me of my foolishness and deceit. It would certainly not have learned the name "Golubchik" so easily.

Besides all this, the "love nest" swarmed with various of Lutetia's friends. They were all made of porcelain and wax. And I drew no distinctions between any of them: the cats, the wallpaper, the parrot and the friends. Lutetia was the only one I still recognized. I was a prisoner, thrice and four times a prisoner. And twice a day I returned voluntarily to my sweet, hateful, alluring prison.

One evening I remained there—it could not have been otherwise! I stayed the night there. Over the parrot's cage hung a covering of red plush. The energetic cats purred comfortably in their baskets. And I slept, no longer a prisoner, but a man chained for all eternity; chained in Lutetia's arms. Poor Golubchik!

In the early morning I woke up, happy and yet unhappy. I felt ensnared and depraved, and yet I still had not lost my feeling for cleanness and decency. But that feeling, my friends, as tender as a breath of air upon a summer's morning, was stronger, far stronger, than the strong wind of sin which raged around me. And it was under the influence of that feeling that I left Lutetia's house. I did not know whether I ought to feel happy or sad. And beset by this doubt, I strode, without thought or plan in my head, through the early streets of Paris.

•   •   •

Lutetia cost money, I very soon discovered that. (All women cost money, especially those who are in love; they cost even more than those who are loved.) And I thought that Lutetia loved me. I was grateful that someone in the world loved me. Besides, Lutetia was the only person who wholly believed in my Krapotkin—who believed in my new existence, yes, even confirmed it. But I was determined not to make any sacrifices for her; only for myself would I make sacrifices. For myself, for the false Golubchik, the real Krapotkin.

So there began a terrible confusion—not in my soul— that had already existed long—but in my private, my material affairs. I began to spend money—with both hands, as one says. Actually, Lutetia herself did not need so much. I myself needed it; I needed it for her. And she began to spend it, senselessly and with that hungry accursed delight with which women always spend the money of their husbands and lovers—almost as though they see in the money which one pays for them, which one even squanders for them, a certain measure of the feeling which their loving men have for them. So I needed money. Very soon. Very much. I went, as was my duty, to my sympathetic chief— his name was Solovejczyk, Michael Nikolajevitch Solovejczyk.

"What have you to report to me?" he asked. It was getting on towards nine o'clock in the evening, and it seemed to me that there was no one else, not a soul, in the great white house. It was very still, and one could hear, as if from an infinite distance, the confused noises of the great city. The whole room was dark. The single lamp with a green shade, standing on Solovejczyk's desk, looked like a bright green core in the surrounding darkness.

"I need money," I said, hidden in the gloom and therefore more boldly than I had intended.

"For the money which you need," he answered, "you must work. We have several jobs for you. It is only a question of whether you are capable—or rather, of whether you are willing to be capable—of carrying out these jobs."

"I am ready for anything," I said. "That is why I came here."

"I do not believe it," said Solovejczyk. "I have not known you long, but I do not believe it. Do you know what this work entails? It entails a vile betrayal—a vile betrayal, I tell you. The betrayal of defenseless people." He paused a while. Then he said: "And of defenseless women. . . ."

"I am used to it. In our profession . . . "

He cut me short. "I know the profession," he said and bent his head. He began to search among the papers which lay before him; and the only sounds in the room were the rustling of paper and the slow ticking of the clock upon the wall.

"Sit down!" said Solovejczyk.

I sat down, and now my face was in the light of the green lamp, opposite his. He raised his eyes and stared fixedly at me. His eyes were dead, there was something blind in them, something comfortless and already far away. I held out against those eyes, although I was afraid of them, for there was nothing to be read in them, no thoughts, no feelings; and yet I knew that they were not blind, on the contrary they were exceedingly sharp. I knew very well that they were observing me, but I was unable to discover the reflex which every observing eye naturally reveals. Indeed, Solovejczyk was the only person whom I have ever found to possess that faculty; that is, the faculty of masking the eyes in the same way as many people can mask their faces.

I watched him. It lasted seconds, minutes; to me it seemed hours. The hair over his temple shone faintly gray, and the muscles along his chin rippled incessantly. It looked as though he were chewing over his reflections. At last he got up, walked across to the window, pulled the curtain back a little and beckoned to me. I came over to him. "Look there," he said, and pointed at a figure on the opposite side of the street. "Do you know him?" I strained my eyes, I peered through the darkness, but all I could see was a smallish, well-dressed man, with a turned-up fur collar and brown hat, and a black stick in his right hand. "Do you recognize him?" asked Solovejczyk again. "No," I said. "Well, we will wait a bit!" Good, we waited. In a short while the man began to walk up and down. After he had taken about twenty paces, a flash went through me. My eyes had not recognized him, my brain had not remembered him, but it flashed into my heart, my blood began to pulse faster. It was suddenly as though my muscles, my hands, my fingertips, my hair, had retained the memory which had been denied to my brain. It was *he*. It was the

same half dragging, half tripping gait which once, when I
was still young and innocent, I had noticed, in a fraction of
a second and in spite of my inexperience, in Odessa. That
was the first and only time in my life when I had seen that
a limp could be graceful and that a foot could disguise itself
as otherwise only a face can. And so I recognized the man
on the opposite side of the street. It was none other than
Lakatos.

"Lakatos!" I said.

"You see!" said Solovejczyk, and stepped back from the
window.

We sat down again opposite one another, exactly as we
had sat before. With his gaze lowered to the papers on the
desk, Solovejczyk said: "You have known Lakatos a long
time?"

"A very long time," I replied. "He is always meeting
me. I would almost say, he is always meeting me in the
decisive hours of my life."

"He will often meet you again—probably," said
Solovejczyk. "I rarely believe, and only very unwillingly, in
the supernatural. But with Lakatos, who visits me from
time to time, I cannot avoid a certain superstitious feeling."

I was silent. What could I have said? It seemed to me
inexorably clear that I had been helplessly caught. A prisoner of Solovejczyk's? A prisoner of Lutetia's? A prisoner,
even, of Lakatos's?

After a pause Solovejczyk said: "He will betray you and
perhaps destroy you."

I picked up the papers containing my orders, a considerable bundle, and went.

"*Auf Wiedersehen,* until next Thursday," said Solovejczyk.

"If I *am* to see you again," I answered.

My heart was heavy.

When I left the house Lakatos was no longer to be seen. Far and wide—no Lakatos, although I searched thoroughly for him, anxiously even. I was afraid of him, and so I sought him anxiously. But I felt already, while I was trying to hunt him out, that I should not find him. Yes, I was certain that I would not find him.

How can one find the Devil by searching for him? He comes, he appears unhoped for, he vanishes. He vanishes, and he is always there.

●   ●   ●

From that hour I no longer felt safe from him. But it was not from him alone that I felt unsafe, it was from the whole world. Who was Solovejczyk? Who was Lutetia? What was Paris? Who was I myself?

More than all the others, I feared myself. Was it my own will which still decided my day, my night, and all my actions? Who was driving me to do what I did at that time? Did I love Lutetia? Did I not only love my passion, or rather my need to confirm myself, my humanity so to speak, through my passion? Who and what was I really—I, Golubchik? If Lakatos were there, I should cease to be

Krapotkin, that seemed certain. Suddenly it became clear
to me that I could be neither Golubchik nor Krapotkin.
Soon I was spending half my days and nights with Lutetia.
I had long ago ceased to hear what she said to me. She only
spoke of unimportant things. I merely noticed many
expressions which had hitherto been unknown to me, the
cadence of words and sentences. Concerning my progress
in French, I had much to thank her for. For, helpless as I
was during those days, I never forgot that a "command of
languages" might prove valuable to me—as Solovejczyk
had once suggested. Well, after a few weeks I had a complete command of French. At home I sometimes dipped
into English, German, Italian books; I stupefied myself
with them, and I imagined that through them I was really
enjoying an existence, a real existence. For example, I read
English newspapers in the hotel lounge. And while I
read them it seemed to me as though I were a fellow
countryman of the white-haired, bespectacled English
colonel over in the opposite armchair. For half an hour I
persuaded myself that I was an Englishman, a colonel from
the Colonies. And why shouldn't I be an English colonel?
Was I Golubchik? Was I Krapotkin? Who and what was
I really?

Every moment I was afraid of meeting Lakatos. He
might come into the hotel lounge. He might come into
the great showrooms of the fashionable dressmaker where
I sometimes went to fetch Lutetia. He might betray me
every moment. He had me in his hand. He might even

betray me to Lutetia—and that would be the worst. In proportion as my fear for Lakatos increased, grew also my passion for Lutetia. It was a sublimated passion, a passion, so to speak, of the second degree. For in reality, during those weeks, it was no longer a true love, it was a flight to passion, just as the doctors today call certain symptoms in women "a flight to sickness." Yes, it was a flight to passion. I was only safe, sure of myself, sure of my own identity, during those hours when I held and loved Lutetia's body. I loved it, not because it was her body, but because it was to a certain extent a refuge, a cell, a sanctuary, safe and secure from Lakatos.

Unfortunately there now happened what needs must have happened sooner or later. Lutetia, who believed as implicitly in my inexhaustible wealth as she would have liked to have believed in her rag-and-bone merchant story, needed money and more money. She needed more and more money. After a few weeks it became clear that she was just as mercenary as she was beautiful. Oh, not that she had tried secretly to put money by, in the way which characterizes so many middle-class women. No! She really spent it. She spent it!

She was like most women of her kind. She did not want to "use up" anything. But *something* in her wished to make use of opportunities, of all opportunities. Weak she was, and immeasurably vain. With women vanity is not only a passive weakness, it is also an extremely active passion, such as only games are with men. Again and again they keep giving birth to this passion; they incite it and at the same time are incited by it. Lutetia's passion dragged me with it. Until then I had never dreamed how much a single woman could spend—and that always in the belief that it is only what is "absolutely necessary." Until then I had never dreamed how powerless a loving man is against the foolishness of a woman. And at that time I was striving to be a loving man; which amounted to the same thing as being really in love. It was just the foolish and unnecessary things that she did which appeared to me to be both necessary and natural. And I will admit that her foolishness flattered me and at the same time confirmed my sham princely existence—for I needed such confirmation. I needed all this outward confirmation: clothes for me and Lutetia, the servility of the tailors who measured me in the hotel with careful fingers as though I were a fragile idol; who scarcely had the courage to touch my shoulders and legs with the tape measure. Just because I was a Golubchik I needed all that which would have wearied a Krapotkin: the menial look in the porter's eyes, the obsequious bowing of the waiters and servants, of whom I saw little more than their faultlessly shaved necks. And money—money I needed, too.

·   ·   ·

I began to earn as much as possible. I earned a lot—and I need not tell you how. Sometimes I remained a whole week hidden from Lutetia and the rest of the world. At such times I mingled with our political refugees. I visited the offices of unimportant little publications and miserable newspapers. I was even shameless enough to accept small loans from the victims I was tracking down; not because I needed the paltry sums of money, but in order to make it seem that I needed the money. In bare little rooms I shared the scanty meals of the hunted, the outcast, the hungry. I was debased enough now and again to attempt the seduction of refugee women who, often happily and sometimes from a sort of tragic sense of duty, gave themselves to a companion in distress. All in all, I was what I had always been, by birth and nature—a scoundrel. To a certain extent, I even proved to myself during those days that I was a scoundrel beyond redemption.

I was lucky. The Devil guided my every footstep. When I visited Solovejczyk on the appointed evenings, I could tell him more than most of my other colleagues. And I perceived from the growing contempt with which he treated me that I was rendering valuable services. "I underestimated your intelligence," he said to me once. "After hearing of your foolishness in Petersburg, I thought you were a petty rascal. My respects to you, Golubchik! I shall pay you well."—For the first time he had called me Golubchik, and he knew well enough that for me that name was like a thrust with a dagger. I took my money, a great deal of money, changed, drove back to my hotel, saw the backs and necks of the staff, saw Lutetia again, saw the nightclubs, the common and superior faces of the waiters, and forgot everything, everything. I was a prince. I even forgot the dreadful Lakatos.

●　　●　　●

I forgot him unjustly.

One mild spring morning I was sitting in the lounge of the hotel, and although the room had no windows it felt as though the sun were streaming in though every pore in the walls. I was bright and cheerful, without a thought in my head, entirely given up to the loathsome contentment with which life filled me. When suddenly Lakatos appeared. He was as gay as the spring itself. He was almost anticipating summer. He came in like a fragment of spring, detached from the rest of nature; wearing a far too light overcoat, a flowered cravat, and a gray top hat; swinging in his right hand the little cane which I knew so well. He addressed me alternately as "Highness" and "Prince," and sometimes he even said, in the manner of small menials: "Your most gracious Highness!" Suddenly the whole of that bright morning darkened for me. How had I been faring all this long time, Lakatos asked me—so loudly, that everyone in the lounge heard it and even the porter in his office. I was monosyllabic. I scarcely answered—for fear, but also out of pride. "So your dear father recognized you?" he asked me softly, while he bent so close to me that I could smell his lilies-of-the-valley scent and the brilliantine which was wafted in heavy waves from his mustache. And I could see plainly a reddish shimmer in his bright brown eyes.

"Yes," I said and leaned back.

"Then you will be pleased to hear," he said, "what I have to tell you."

He paused. I said nothing.

"Your dear brother arrived here yesterday," he said calmly. "He is living in his house. He has a permanent residence in Paris. As every year, he intends to remain here for a few months. I believe you are now reconciled with him?"

"Not yet," I said, and could scarcely conceal my impatience and tenor.

"Well," said Lakatos, "I hope that will soon come to pass. In any case, I am always at your service."

"Thank you," I said. He got up, bowed low and went. I remained seated.

·   ·   ·

But not for long. I drove straight to Lutetia. She was not at home. I drove to the dressmaker's shop. With a large bouquet I thrust my way in, as with a couched lance. I was able to speak with her for a few moments. She knew nothing of Krapotkin's arrival. I left the shop. I sat down in a café and hoped that by concentrated thought I might arrive at some brilliant inspiration. But all my thoughts were contaminated with jealousy, hatred, passion, vengefulness. Soon I persuaded myself that it

would be best to go to Solovejczyk and ask him to send
me back to Russia. Then, once more, fear overcame me;
fear of losing my present life, fear of losing Lutetia, my
stolen name, everything that contributed to my existence.
I thought for a moment of killing myself, but I had a horror of death. It was much easier, much better, but in no
way pleasanter, to kill the Prince. To rid the world of him!
Once for all to be free from that ridiculous youth, that
really ridiculous and useless fool! But in the same
moment, and with the ruthless logic dictated by my conscience, I said to myself that if he were a useless fool *I*
was still worse, being both evil and harmful. But scarcely
a minute later it seemed clear to me that the cause of my
evilness and harmfulness was he alone, he, that superfluous creature, and that to kill him would be ethically
justifiable. For, in destroying him, I should also destroy the
cause of my corruption, and then I should be free to
become a decent citizen, to atone, to repent, even to
become a respectable Golubchik. But even while I was
thinking of all this, I realized that I was far from possessing the necessary determination to commit a murder. At
that time, my friends, I was not nearly clean enough to be
able to kill. Whenever I considered destroying a certain
person, it was synonymous to me, to my mentality, with
the decision to ruin him in some way or other. We spies
are no murderers. We only prepare the circumstances
which must inevitably lead to a man's death. I, too,
thought no differently; I was incapable of thinking differ-

ently. I was a scoundrel by birth and nature, as I have already told you. . . .

Among the many people whom, at that time, it was my loathsome duty to betray and deliver up, there was a certain Jewess by the name of Channa Lea Rifkin, from Radzivillov. Never shall I forget her name or her face. Two of her brothers had been arrested in Russia and condemned to Katorga on account of an attempted assassination of the Governor of Odessa. They had already been three years in Siberia, as I knew from the documents of the case. The sister had succeeded in escaping in time and taking with her a third brother, a half-crippled youth who had to sit all day in a wheelchair. He could only move his right arm and right leg. It was said that he was an extremely gifted mathematician and physicist and that he possessed an extraordinary memory. The plans and formula, with the aid of which explosives could be made without using complicated apparatus, had all emanated from him. Brother and sister lived with Swiss friends, French-Swiss from Geneva, a shoemaker and his wife. Russian refugees often met together in the shoemaker's workshop. I myself had been there several times. This brave Jewish girl was determined to return to Russia and rescue her brothers. She took all the responsibility on herself. Their mother was dead, their father was ill. And she had three young sisters to keep. In numerous petitions to the Russian Embassy she had declared herself ready to return to Russia if only they would give her the assurance that her innocent brothers, who had only been implicated in the plot through her, would be freed. For us, that is, for the Russian police, it was a question of getting hold of her at any price; but, at the same time, we had to prevent the Embassy from giving any official promises. Besides, an embassy could not, dared not, do such a thing. But Channa Lea was "needed" urgently. "We need her" was written in the reports.

Up to the day when I received the visit from Lakatos, it had nevertheless been impossible for me, a scoundrel by birth and nature, to betray these people. These people—I mean the girl and her brother—were the only ones, among all the Russians whom it was my duty to destroy, who still stirred the remnants of my conscience. If, at that time, I could possibly have understood the meaning of a deadly sin, those two people were the only ones who could have brought me that understanding. From that gentle, tender girl—if there are Jewish angels, they must look like her—in whose face the hardness and the sweetness were so compounded that one seemed to see clearly that hardness was a sister of sweetness—from that gentle and yet strong girl there emanated a magical power—a magical power—I cannot express it otherwise. She was not beautiful, in the sense that beauty is understood in this world, where we call seductiveness beauty. No, she was not beautiful, but this small, insignificant Jewess touched the depths of my soul, and she even touched my senses; for when I looked at her it was as though I were hearing a song. Yes, it was as though

I did not see her, but only heard something beautiful, strange, unknown, and yet very intimate. Sometimes, during those still hours when the crippled brother sat on the edge of the sofa, reading a book propped up on a high chair, when the canaries in their cage trilled triumphantly, and a narrow strip of sun crept across the bare wooden floor, I would sit opposite the brave girl, watching her silently, studying her pale, broad, innocent face, in which the sufferings of all our Russian Jews lay plain to read, and I would be on the point of telling her everything. I was certainly not the only spy who had been sent to her, and who knows how many of my colleagues I might not have met at her house. (For we seldom knew one another.) But I am convinced, even today, that all or most of them felt like me. That child had weapons against which we were powerless. Our duty was to entice her back to Russia under the pretense that her brothers would be set free; but it was naturally not so easy to deceive her, and she would never have trusted any promise other than that signed by the ambassador of the Czar. Or, failing that, it might perhaps have sufficed to learn from her the names of all her confederates who had stayed behind in Russia. And, my friends, I told you before that I was a scoundrel by birth and nature. Yet in the presence of that young girl my vileness melted away, and I sometimes felt as though my heart were crying, as though, in the most literal sense, it were slowly thawing.

•　　•　　•

The months passed, and summer came. I thought of traveling away somewhere with Lutetia. But one day there appeared in my hotel a white-haired, soberly clad old man. With his thick, silvery hair, with his imposing and carefully combed white beard, with his black ebony stick, whose gleaming silver handle seemed fashioned out of the same material as his hair, he seemed to me like a high and macabre dignitary at the court of the Czar. So, I imagined to myself, must the officials of the Imperial court look when they perform their functions at the deathbed and the burial of a Czar. But after I had looked at him for some time, he seemed suddenly to recognize me. His face, his thick hair, his beard and his voice rose up from a long-forgotten past. And in a flash, when he said to me: "I am glad to see you again after so many years, Herr Golubchik!" I, too, knew who he was. He might be very old. But once I had heard his voice behind a door, and for a second I had seen his silver and black figure in a dark corridor. It was the secretary of the old Prince. Many, many years before—how long ago that was!—he had come to the owner of my *pension* and paid for me. He scarcely held out his hand to me. For a fraction of a second I felt three cold, shrunken, almost stony fingertips. I begged him to sit down. As though he were unwilling to do my chair too much honor, he seated himself on the extreme edge, so that he had to support himself with his stick between his knees in order to avoid sliding off. Between two fingers he held his black top hat. He began immediately, as the Latin phrase goes, *in media*

res. "Herr Golubchik," he said, "the young Prince is here.
The old gentleman may also stay here a while on his journey to the South. Unjustifiably and—to use no stronger
word—in a dishonorable way, you have caused their
Highnesses a great deal of unpleasantness. You call yourself
Krapotkin here. You maintain certain relations with a
young lady. She, too, has several names. The young Prince
has now at last made up his mind no longer to tolerate
such behavior.—It is a piece of madness. But that is by the
way.—The young Prince is very generous. Consider for a
moment and then tell me straight out how much you
require to disappear, once and forever, from our sight.
Already once, you have had an experience of how great
our power is. If you remain obstinate, you will be faced
with a far greater danger than any of those poor wretches
whom you are pursuing. Of course, I wish to say nothing
against your profession. It is, shall we say, scarcely honorable, but extremely necessary, extremely necessary—in the
interests of the State. Our country naturally needs people
like you. But to the family whom I have had the honor to
serve and represent for more than forty years, you are
merely obnoxious. The Krapotkin family is prepared to
give you a new start in America, or even in Russia if you
wish it. So consider, how much do you want?" At these
words the silvery-haired old man drew a heavy gold watch
from his pocket. He held it in his hand, somewhat like a
doctor who is taking his patient's pulse. I deliberated.
I really deliberated. It seemed to me hopeless to make

evasions in front of this man, or even in front of myself; and it seemed to me equally hopeless to play for a superfluous and highly ridiculous breathing space. His watch ticked relentlessly. How long would he wait?

I had reached no decision. But the good spirit which never leaves us, not even when we are scoundrels by birth and nature, suddenly brought back the memory of Channa Lea. And I said: "I do not need money. I need a favor from the Prince. If he is as powerful as you say, he can do it for me. Can I see him?"

"Immediately!" said the old man. He returned his watch to his pocket and stood up. "Come with me!"

The private coach of Prince Krapotkin—the genuine one—was standing outside the hotel. We drove off. We drew up in front of the Prince's private house. It was a villa in the Bois de Boulogne, and in the lackey at the door, who wore a beard like the secretary, I thought I recognized that same servant whom I had seen so many, many years ago in the summer residence of the old Prince at Odessa.

I was announced. The secretary left me. I waited for at least half an hour. I sat, anxious and depressed, downstairs in the anteroom, as I had once sat in the anteroom of the old Prince. But I was far different from the Golubchik of those days. Then, the world had stood open before me; today, I was a Golubchik who had lost the world. I knew it. And yet it mattered little to me. I had only to force myself to think of Channa Lea, and it mattered not at all to me.

At last I was ushered into the Prince's room. He looked exactly the same as he had that time when I watched him through a crack in the wall and saw him in a *chambre separée* with Lutetia. Yes, he looked exactly the same. How shall I describe him to you? You know the type: an aristocratic, impotent windbag. He looked not unlike a used-up piece of soap. So pale and insipid was his skin. He looked like a piece of used-up yellow soap with a thin black mustache. I hated him as I had always hated him.

He was pacing backwards and forwards across the room, and when I entered he never stopped for a moment. He paced on, as though the old man had brought, not me, but a doll. Neither did he turn to me, but to the secretary, and asked: "How much?"

"I would like to deal with you myself," I said.

"I would not," he answered and never paused for a moment in his pacing. He looked at the secretary. "Deal with him!"

"I do not need money," I said. "If you are really as powerful as you say, you can have everything you want of me if you will free two men from Katorga and a girl from punishment. Immediately. If you free them within a week!"

"Very well," said the secretary. "But until then, you will hide yourself as far as possible. Give me the facts."

I gave him the facts about the brothers Rifkin. In a few days I would be informed of the result.

·   ·   ·

I waited a few days. I waited, I must say, with the greatest impatience, with a sort of moral impatience. I purposely say "with moral impatience," because at that time a longing for repentance overcame me, and I believed that the moment had arrived in which I could atone for all my vileness with one so-called "good deed."

I waited. I waited.

At last I was summoned to the Prince's private house.

The dignified old secretary received me, sitting. He made a gesture of invitation, but only a very fleeting one, not even inviting me to be seated, but rather as though brushing me away, as one disposes of a fly.

In defiance, I sat down and crossed my legs. In defiance, too, I said: "Where is the Prince?"

"To you, not at home," answered the old man mildly. "The Prince asked me to tell you that he has no time to bother with political affairs. He will have nothing to do with such sordid matters. Neither will he bargain with you. In addition to that, you would be in a position to denounce him, as you have already done once before, and to represent him as a protector of persons hostile to the State. You understand. We can only offer you money. If you will not accept that, we have other means of removing you from Paris. You can scarcely be as indispensable to our country as all that. There are certainly others who are just as useful, if not more so, than you."

"I will not take money," I replied, "and I shall stay in Paris." At that, I thought of my sympathetic chief,

Solovejczyk. I would explain everything to him. But I had completely forgotten the dead stare he had given me on the last occasion I saw him. I imagined that Solovejczyk favored me, was even fond of me.

I determined to go to him immediately.

I got up and said solemnly (today it seems to me ridiculous): "A real Krapotkin"—I emphasised the word: *real*—"accepts no compensation money. A false one offers it."

I expected a gesture, a word of indignation from the mouth of the old man. But he never moved. He did not even look at me. He only stared at the black surface of his desk, as though there were papers lying there, as though he were reading in the wood, and as though there stood written there the sentence which he spoke a few seconds later.

"Go," he said, without lifting his gaze, let alone getting up himself, "and do what seems fitting to you."

The word "fitting" made me redden.

I went, without a word. It was raining, and I bade the flunkey fetch me a cab. I still felt myself a prince, although I already knew that I was once more a Golubchik; at the most I could only remain a Krapotkin for a few more days.

But I was happy, my friends, in spite of the knowledge that in a little while I should have to return to my old existence and my rightful name. Believe me, I was happy. And if anything grieved me then, it was the fact that I had been unable to help the Jewess Rifkin. For I had indeed thought that I had found an opportunity to atone for all the evil I had done. Well!—I had least saved my own existence, and perhaps even purified it a little.

•　　•　　•

When I returned to the hotel—it was getting late and solitary lights were already burning in the hall—I was informed that a gentleman was waiting for me in the writing room.

I thought it must be Lakatos, and went, without saying a word, into the writing room. But the figure which rose from the broad sofa behind a table was far from being my friend Lakatos; it was, to my astonishment, the fashionable dressmaker, the creator of "creations."

There was a sort of twilight in the writing room, which was strengthened rather than weakened by the green-shaded lamps which stood on the various writing tables. The lamps seemed to me like illuminated poison bottles.

In this curious light the broad pale face of the dressmaker looked to me like dough in the oven, dough which is rising. Yes, the nearer he came to me, the greater grew his pulpy face, greater and broader even in comparison to his over-large, flapping, effeminate clothes. He bowed before me, and it was as though a sort of square ball were doing obeisance to me. I was no longer inclined to believe that the dressmaker was a real living being.

"Prince," he said, as he laboriously raised his angular and yet spherical body, "may I discuss a small detail with you?"

It seemed to me ridiculous that someone should still address me as "Prince," but nevertheless it flattered me. I begged the man to say what was on his mind.

"A mere detail, Prince," he reassured me, "an absurd trifle." And at that he described a complete circle in the air with his fat doughy hand. "It is a question of a small debt. The matter is distressing to me, even repugnant. It concerns Mademoiselle Lutetia's clothes."

"What clothes?" I asked.

"Two months have already passed," said Monsieur Charron. "And Mademoiselle Lutetia is an extraordinary person, girl—lady, I mean. It is sometimes difficult to get on with her. She is, I must say, a real lady, not like the others. And although she is the daughter of one of my ordinary, what am I saying, of one of my *greatest* colleagues, she has the same tastes (quite rightly) as the most exclusive of our customers. I must confess, Your Highness, I must confess that I have sold her, that is, to Mademoiselle Lutetia, three of my best models, which she herself had displayed. But I would never have come to disturb Your Highness, were I not momentarily suffering from certain acute financial embarrassments."

"How much?" I asked, like a real prince.

"Eight thousand!" said Charron promptly.

"Good!" I said—like a real prince. And I dismissed him.

After he had gone, I drove straight to Lutetia. Eight thousand francs, my friends—that was no trifle for me, a wretched penniless spy. Of course, I should perhaps have done nothing. But—was I not still in love? Was I not still a prisoner?

I went to Lutetia. She was sitting at a table laid for supper and waiting for me, as usual—as she even did on the evenings when I could not come—as befits a so-called "well-bred" young woman.

I gave her the customary kiss, which a man is in duty bound to give to the woman he keeps. It was a duty kiss, such as the great condescend to give.

I ate, without any appetite, and I must admit that, for all my love, I observed Lutetia's healthy appetite with some ill-will. I was, at that time, petty enough to think of the eight thousand francs. A great many other things, too, came into my mind. I thought of myself, the real Golubchik. A few hours earlier I had been glad to be a real Golubchik again. Yet now, with Lutetia at the same table, the thought that I was to be a Golubchik once more filled me with bitterness. But at the same time I was still somehow a Krapotkin, and I had eight thousand francs to pay. As a Krapotkin, I had to pay them. Suddenly I felt embittered at the amount of the sum, I who had never counted or calculated. There are, my friends, certain moments in which the money one has to pay for a passion seems almost as important as the passion itself—and its object. I never gave a thought to the fact that I had wooed and won Lutetia, the beloved of my heart, with shameful and villainous lies. On the contrary, I used it as a reproach against her, that she believed my lies and lived on them. A strange, unknown fury rose up within me. I loved Lutetia. But I was angry with her. Soon it seemed to me, while we were still eating, that she alone was responsible for my debt. I searched, I scrutinized, I delved for faults in her. I discovered that it was tantamount to a betrayal to have told me nothing about the clothes.

Therefore I said slowly, while I folded up my serviette equally slowly: "Monsieur Charron came to see me today."

"Swine," said Lutetia simply.

"Why?" I asked.

"Old swine," said Lutetia.

"Why?" I repeated.

"Pah! What do you know about it!" said Lutetia.

"I am supposed to pay eight thousand francs for you," I said. "Why didn't you tell me?"

"I needn't tell you everything," she replied.

"Yes, everything," I said.

"Not little things!" said Lutetia. She propped her clasped hands under her chin and looked at me, pugnaciously and almost evilly. "Not everything," she repeated.

"Why not?" I asked.

"Well."

"What do you mean: Well?"

"I'm a woman," she said.

What an argument! I thought—and pulled myself together, as the phrase goes, and said:

"I have never doubted that you were a woman!"

"But you have never understood it!" she said. "Let us talk practically and sensibly," I said, still calm. "Why didn't you tell me about your clothes?"

"A trifle!" she answered. "What did they cost?"

"Eight thousand," I said.

At that I feared—although I had already determined to be a plain Golubchik—that I had not spoken as a Prince Krapotkin would have spoken in similar circumstances.

"A trifle!" she said. "I am a woman. I need clothes!"

"Why didn't you tell me before?"

"I am a woman!"

"I know that."

"You don't! Otherwise you wouldn't waste time discussing all this."

"You could have spared me Charron's visit," I said. "I dislike such things. I hate surprises." I was still talking like a prince—although my mind was fully occupied with the eight thousand francs.

"Do you want to go on quarrelling with me?" asked Lutetia. And there began to glow in her beautiful, soulless eyes, which at that moment reminded me of glass marbles, an angry little fire, such as you, my friends, will have seen in the eyes of your wives—at certain times. If fire has sex, I believe that there is a quite definite feminine fire. It has no reason, no visible cause. I suspect that it is always glowing in a woman's soul and sometimes it blazes up and burns in her eyes: a fine and yet an evil little fire. As one regards it. At all events, I am afraid of it.

With that wanton violence which with a woman is so often playacting and equally often is so very real, Lutetia got up, threw down her serviette, and said once more:

"I won't stand it any longer! I have had enough!" And as though she had not already said it several times, she repeated: "You will never realize it!—I am a woman!"

I, too, got up. I thought, inexperienced as I then was, that a woman could be soothed and appeased by a tender caress. On the contrary, my friends, the very opposite is the case! Scarcely had I stretched out a propitiatory hand than sweet Lutetia, the beloved of my heart, hammered her clenched fists into my face. At the same time she stamped with both feet—a curious characteristic which we men lack when we hit out—and she screamed: "You will pay— pay, tomorrow—tomorrow morning—I demand it!"

'What would a Prince Krapotkin have done then, my friends? Probably he would have said: "Certainly!" and walked out. But I, who was now a Golubehik, said: "No!" and stayed.

Suddenly Lutetia laughed gaily, the sort of laugh that is called a "theatrical laugh" but is not a theatrical laugh at all. For the women on the stage simply imitate the women in real life, themselves. Where does so-called life stop and where does the so-called theater begin?

So she laughed, the beloved of my heart. It lasted a considerable time. But everything has an end, as you know, my friends. After Lutetia had laughed to an end, she became suddenly quite serious, almost tragic, and said in a quiet voice: "If you don't pay, your cousin will."

It frightened me when Lutetia said that; yes, it frightened me, although I had nothing more to fear. If my

so-called brother had already been with Lutetia, my real
identity could not be kept hidden from her much longer.
And why—I asked myself—should it be kept hidden from
her? Had I not longed, just before I came there, to throw
off my horrible disguise and become once more a plain
Golubchik?

So why was I now distressed again at having to give up
my confused and confusing existence? Did I love Lutetia
so much? Was the sight of her alone sufficient to overthrow
all my resolution? Did she attract me now, at this very
moment? Could I not see that she was lying, could I not
see that she was venal? Yes, I saw everything, and I despised
her for it, too. And perhaps, if it had not been my false
brother who had again, just here again, crossed my path, I
would have left her. I had been magnanimous to him, I had
refused his money—and lo! his miserable power once
more stood in my way.

Of course I could never hope to raise that enormous
sum of money, nor even a third of it. What wouldn't I
have had to do in order to obtain, all at once, even three
thousand francs, so that I could at least begin payments?
And could I, even if I did pay, prevent Lutetia from learn-
ing who I really was? If only I had the money, I thought in
my infatuation, I would tell her who I was and that I had
committed the very worst of my infamous deeds for her
sake, and also that a Golubchik could hold his own with
any woman against a Krapotkin. So I thought. And
although I knew that she lied and that she was a creature

without a trace of conscience, I credited her with the generosity not only to accept, but also to treasure, my sincerity. I even believed that sincerity would move her. But women—and, to be honest, men too—may be partial to genuinely sincere people, yet nevertheless they dislike hearing the sincere confessions of liars and deceivers.

But to continue with my story. I asked Lutetia whether she had already seen my cousin. No—she said, he had only written to her. But sooner or later she was expecting a visit from him, probably in the dressmaker's shop. "You will send him away immediately!" I said. "I don't like you seeing him!" "It makes not the slightest difference to me whether you like it or not. Besides, I'm tired of you!" "Do you love him?" I asked, without looking at her. I was mad enough to believe that she would answer either yes or no. But she said: "And if I do love him? What then?" "Take care!" I said, "You don't know me, or what I'm capable of." "Of nothing!" she answered, and stepped over to the cage of the repulsive parrot and began tickling the bird's carmine throat. In the next moment, it cackled three times, one after another: Krapotkin, Krapotkin, Krapotkin. Lutetia had taught it that trick. It was as if she already knew everything about me and wished to tell me only through the parrot.

I let the parrot finish speaking, out of politeness, as though it were human. Then I said: "You'll see what I'm capable of!" "Well, show me then," she retorted. And suddenly she fell into a rage, or acted as though she were in a rage. It seemed to me that her hair all at once began to wave, although there was no wind in the room! At the same time, the parrot's feathers ruffled. Lutetia grasped the metal swing on which the horrible bird used to perch—and struck out blindly at me. I felt her blows, they hurt too, although I was very powerful. But far stronger than the blows was the surprise at seeing my well-known beloved Lutetia changed into a sort of deliberate, perfumed hurricane, an entrancing hurricane, which nevertheless provoked me into an attempt to tame her. I gripped her arms, she screamed with pain, the bird screeched shrilly as though it were calling the neighbors to help against me. Lutetia reeled, the blood ebbed from her face, she sank to the carpet. She certainly did not drag me with her, for I was too heavy. But I let myself fall. She encircled me with her arms. And so we lay together, for long hours, in ecstatic hatred.

.   .   .

I got up. It was still deep night, although I could already feel the approach of morning. I let Lutetia lie. I thought she was asleep. But she said in a tender, loving, childish voice: "Promise to come tomorrow to the shop. Protect me from your cousin. I cannot bear him. I love you!"

I went home, through the silent, fading night. I walked carefully, for I expected to meet Lakatos every moment.

It seemed, also, as though I could hear from time to

time a soft, dragging step. Although I was afraid of my friend, I believed that that night I needed him urgently. I needed, so I believed, his advice. And yet I knew that it would be advice from Hell.

•   •   •

The next day, before I went to the dressmaker's—that is, to Lutetia—I drank heavily. And while I befuddled myself, I believed that my brain was gradually growing clearer and clearer and forging cleverer and cleverer plans.

The dressmaker greeted me enthusiastically. His creditors—recognizable at first glance by their gloomy smiles and eloquent silence—were waiting for him in the next room.

I did not know exactly what I was saying. I wanted to see Lutetia. She was standing in her dressing room, between three mirrors, while a designer was trying different stuffs on her, alternately wrapping and unwrapping her, and it looked as though he were martyring her to a slow and elegant death with a hundred pins.

"Has he been here?" I asked, over the oily heads of three youths who were grouped around with materials and pins.

"No. He only sent some flowers!"

I wanted to say something more, but firstly I began to choke, and secondly Lutetia waved to me to leave the room. "This evening," she said.

Monsieur Charron was waiting for me outside the

door. "This afternoon, for certain," I said, in order to avoid having to speak with him further, although I had no great hopes that Solovejczyk would give me the money.

I went out quickly and drove to Solovejczyk.

I knew very well that he was seldom to be found at this hour. His room had two anterooms, each on an opposite side. The anterooms hung on the central room just like two ears on a head. One anteroom was reached through a white door with gilded moldings.—The other, on the opposite side, was curtained off by a heavy green portière. In the first room waited the unsuspecting, those who knew nothing of Solovejczyk's real activities. In the second waited the others, we the initiated. I did not know them all, only a few. Through the portière we could hear everything that Solovejczyk discussed with the unsuspecting. They were mostly ridiculous matters: the export and import of grain, special concessions for hop merchants in the season, extension of passports for the sick, recommendations for businessmen to foreign governments. For us, the initiated, all these things held no interest; but our ears, trained to listen, took in everything. We could easily have talked with one another while we were thus waiting, but none of us could control our professional urge to listen; and so we avoided conversation, which would only have interfered with our listening. Also we mistrusted one another, even avoided one another. As soon as Solovejczyk had finished with the unsuspecting, he drew back the green portière, looked into our anteroom and selected, according to the importance of the person or the case, the first of us to go in. At this point, the other "initiateds" had to go out and along the corridor into the opposite ante-room, the one separated by a door through which one could hear nothing.

That afternoon Solovejczyk arrived late, but the unsus-pecting—with whom he used to talk loudly, often indeed shouting—were soon disposed of. There were six of us waiting to see him. He called me in first.

"You have been drinking," he said. "Sit down."

Friendly as he had never been before, he offered me a cigarette out of a heavy silver box.

I had carefully prepared the beginning of my speech, but his friendliness dazed me and I forgot everything.

"I have nothing special to report," I said. "I have only one request. I need money."

"Of course," said Solovejczyk. "The Prince is here." He blew a cloud of smoke into the air. "Young man," he began, "you will never be able, in the long run, to hold out against this competition. You will fail miserably." He dissected and distended the word "miserably." It was an endless, bound-less "miserably." "You are a person," he continued, "whom I myself"—and for the first time I perceived a sort of van-ity in him—"whom I myself," he repeated, "cannot quite make out. You refuse to accept money. You wanted to get the Rifkins set free. You are gifted, certainly. But you are not complete. How can I express it—you are still a man. You are already a scoundrel—pardon the word; coming from my mouth it is not meant personally, but, so to speak, 'literally.' But you still have human weaknesses. You must decide."

"I have decided," I said.

"Tell me honestly," asked Solovejczyk, "were you really intending to set a trap for the Prince when you asked him to intervene on behalf of the Rifkins?"

"Yes," I said, although, as you know, that was not true.

"I see," said Solovejczyk. "Then you are complete. It would have been useless. The Prince will never let himself be caught. But you can still have the money. And you will bring the little Rifkin to Russia."

"But how?" I asked. "She is suspicious."

"How, is your affair," said Solovejczyk. "You can forge."

I extinguished my cigarette in the black agate ashtray.

"I don't know how to forge," I said helplessly, like a child.

I was lost. Before my eyes stood the brave little Jewess. Before my eyes stood my beloved Lutetia. Before my eyes stood the enemy of my life, young Krapotkin. Before my eyes Lakatos suddenly limped into sight with his dragging foot. All of them, all, so it seemed to me, ruled my life. Only what was it now? Was it still my own life? A great rage against all four surged through me. An equal hatred against all of them, my friends, although I knew exactly how to differentiate between them, although I knew exactly that I really loved the brave Channa Rifkin, that I desired and despised Lutetia, only desiring her because I hoped to win thereby a petty, cheap, miserable triumph over Krapotkin, and that I feared Lakatos as the actual emissary of Satan who had thought out for me, for me especially, a little private devil. A sudden, indescribable, ecstatic desire filled me, the desire to be stronger than all of them, stronger even than my own feelings which bound me to them; to be stronger than my real love for the Jewish girl; stronger than my hatred for Krapotkin; stronger than my desire for Lutetia; stronger than my fear for Lakatos. Yes, I wanted to be stronger even than myself; that was what it really was.

So I plunged into the greatest crime of my life. But I did not yet know how to set about it, in the safest way, and I asked again timidly: "I don't know how to forge."

Solovejczyk looked at me with his dead, pale gray eyes and said: "Perhaps your old friend can advise you. Go out there." And he pointed, not to the door, but to the portière through which I had come in.

•   •   •

One thing is certain, my friends. Fate guides our steps. A reasonable assumption, and as old as Fate itself. We see it sometimes. Mostly we do not wish to see it. I, too, belonged to those who are unwilling to see it, and all too often I closed my eyes tight in order not to see it, just as a child shuts its eyes in the dark so as not to be afraid of the darkness around it. But as for me—perhaps I was accursed, perhaps I was elect—Fate compelled me at every step, and in obvious, almost banal ways, to open my eyes again and again.

When I left the Embassy—it was situated, as you all know, in one of the most fashionable streets, together with several other embassies—I looked out for a *bistro*. For I belong to that numerous class which finds some measure of mental clarity, not in action, but in sitting down in front of a glass. So I looked out for a *bistro*. There was one about forty yards down a side street to the right; it was a so-called *tabac*. And not more than twenty yards farther on was another. I did not want to go into the *tabac,* I wanted to go into the other. So I walked past. But just as I reached the second, I turned around, for no explicable reason, and went back into the *tabac.* I sat down at one of the tiny little tables in the back portion of the shop. Through the glass door which separated me from the buffet I could see cigarette purchasers coming and going. I sat facing the glass door, and so never noticed that behind my back there was another door, an ordinary wooden one. I ordered a brandy and decided to consider my position.

"There you are, old friend," I heard a voice say behind me. I turned around. You will have guessed who it was. It was my friend Lakatos.

I offered him only two fingers, but he squeezed them as though it were my whole hand.

He sat down immediately. He was gay, spruce; his white teeth glistened; his black mustache shimmered bluely; his straw hat was pushed on to one side, over the left ear. I noticed that he was carrying no cane today; for the first time I saw him without his stick. But the thing that caught my attention was his dispatch case, made of red Saffian leather.

"Good news," he said and pointed to the case. "The prizes have been increased."

"What sort of prizes."

"Prizes for enemies of the State," he said, as though it were a question of prizes for runners or bicyclists—as was common at that time.

"I have just come from Monsieur Charron," continued Lakatos. "He is expecting you."

"He can wait!" I said. But I was uneasy.

While Lakatos dipped his pastry in the coffee—I can still remember, it was a French roll, what they call a *croissant*—he added casually: *"Á propos,* you have friends here. The Rifkins."

"Yes," I said brazenly.

"I know," said Lakatos. "The girl must go back to Russia. Hard, very hard, to deliver up such a brave girl." He fell silent and dipped the *croissant* into his coffee again. As he swallowed the soddened pastry, he said: "Two thousand—"and then, after a longer pause—"rubles!"

We said nothing for a few minutes. Suddenly Lakatos stood up, opened the glass door, glanced at the clock over the buffet, and said: "I must go. I'll leave my hat and case here. In ten, at the most fifteen, minutes, I shall be back."

And he was already out of the door.

Opposite me leaned Lakatos's fiery red case. The straw hat lay beside it, like a satellite. The lock on the case glistened like a tightly closed golden mouth. A greedy, covetous mouth.

A professional, but not only a professional, also a sort of supernatural, devilish curiosity compelled me continuously to glance across the table and stare at the dispatch case. I could easily open it before Lakatos returned. Ten minutes, he had said. Through the glass door I could hear the harsh ticking of the clock over the buffet. I was afraid of the case. On either side of the middle lock, which, as I have said, resembled a mouth, there were two smaller locks, and these now looked to me like eyes. I drank two more double brandies, and already the eyes on the case were beginning to wink at me. Still the clock ticked, and time passed, and I believed I suddenly knew how precious time was.

At moments it seemed to me that Lakatos's red case was bowing to me from the chair on which it was propped. At last, when I thought it was about to offer itself to me completely, I stretched out for it. I opened it. Since I could still hear the hard and relentless ticking of the clock, it occurred to me that Lakatos might return any moment, so I went with the case into the lavatory. Should Lakatos come back in the meanwhile, I could always say that I had taken it with me as a precaution. It seemed to me as though I were not just taking it, but actually abducting it.

I opened it with feverish fingers. I should have already known what it contained—how could I not have known,

I who knew so well the Devil and his relationship to me. But we often know things—as was the case with me—by quite other means than through our senses or understanding; and from laziness, cowardice, habit, we guard ourselves against such knowledge. Such were my feelings, too, at that moment. I mistrusted my own knowledge; or rather, I was making a desperate effort to mistrust it.

Some among you, my friends, may perhaps guess what were the papers I found in Lakatos's dispatch case. Those that concerned me I knew well; I knew them from past experience in my profession. They were the stamped and signed passport papers which our people used to give to wretched emigrants in order to lure them back to Russia. By such means, countless people had been delivered up by us to the authorities. The unsuspecting victims journeyed happily home, safe, so they thought, with legal passports. But on the frontier they were arrested, and only after weeks and months of agonizing suspense were they brought before a court, removed to prison, and finally sent to Siberia. The unhappy fools had trusted us—put their faith in people of my type. The stamps were genuine, the signatures were genuine, the photographs were genuine—how could they suspect? Not even the official authorities knew of our shameful methods. On each passport there was a tiny sign which enabled our people at the frontier to distinguish those of the suspected from those of the unsuspected. Of course, those signs escaped the eye of a casual observer. And they were also changed frequently. Sometimes it was a minute pinprick through the passport owner's photograph; then again, half a letter might be missing from the imprint of the round stamp; or else the owner's name would be written in script instead of in ordinary handwriting. Of all these ruses the official authorities knew as little as the victims themselves. Only our people at the frontier knew the fiendish signs. In Lakatos's dispatch case I found a complete set of stamps and ink pads, red and blue and black and violet. I returned to my table and waited.

A few minutes later Lakatos came in and sat down. With some solemnity he drew an envelope from out of his coat pocket and handed it to me without a word. While I was engaged in opening this, which bore the seal of our Embassy, I saw how he took one of the passport papers out of his red leather case, and I heard him order pen and ink. In the document which I read, the Imperial Embassy informed Prince Krapotkin that, by the special clemency of the Czar, the brothers Rifkin had been released, and the sister—Channa Lea Rifkin—had no longer any danger to fear, should she choose to return to Russia. I was horrified, my friends, I was filled with a deep, sickening horror. But I did not stand up to go away. I did not even push the document back to Lakatos. I only watched how Lakatos, who took not the slightest notice of me, slowly, carefully, comfortably, in his beautiful, copperplate, official handwriting, made out a passport for the Jewess Rifkin.

My friends! Even as I tell you this, I tremble with self-hatred and contempt. But at the time I was as dumb as a fish and as indifferent as a hangman before his hundredth execution. I believe that a virtuous man would be as little able to explain his noblest act as a scoundrel of my type his foulest. I knew that it was a question of destroying the noblest woman I had ever met. I saw already, with my practiced eye, the secret, devilish pinprick over the name. I did not tremble, I did not move. I thought of the unhappy Lutetia. And, as true as I am a scoundrel, I was only afraid of one thing: I would have to go myself to the Rifkins and tell the girl and her brother the happy, fatal news. I was so terrified at the thought of this that, curiously enough—or rather, shamefully enough—I felt free of any guilt when Lakatos, after he had carefully blotted his signature in the passport, stood up and said: "I am going to her myself. You need only write two lines: 'The bearer of this is a friend. Farewell, and *auf Wiedersehen* in Russia. Krapotkin.'" At the same time he pushed the ink pot and paper across to me and pressed the pen into my hand. And, my friends—do you still permit me to call you "friends"?—I signed. My hand wrote. Never before had it written so quickly.

Without drying the ink, Lakatos picked up the paper. He waved it in his hand like a flag. Under his left arm glowed the red dispatch case.

•   •   •

All this happened in a far shorter time than it takes to tell. Scarcely five minutes later I jumped up, paid hastily and ran out of the door in search of a cab. But no cab came. Instead of a cab I saw a lackey from the Embassy hurrying straight towards me. Solovejczyk summoned me.

Of course, I knew immediately that Lakatos had told him where I was to be found. But instead of making some excuse and searching further for a cab, I followed the servant and went to Solovejczyk.

I was the only one sitting in the anteroom of the initiated, but he kept me waiting a long time. Ten minutes passed, ten eternities; then he called me. I began immediately: "I must go. A precious human life may be lost. I must go!"

"Of whom are you talking," he asked slowly. "Of the Rifkins," I said. "I have never heard of them, I know nothing about them," said Solovejczyk. "Stay where you are! You needed money. Here! For special services." He gave me my reward. My friends. One who has never taken a reward for a betrayal may perhaps think of "blood money" as an empty phrase. I not. I not.

• • •

I ran out, without a hat. I hailed a cab. Every moment I drummed with my fists on the cabby's back. More and more violently he slashed and cracked his whip. 'We arrived at the shoemaker's shop. I jumped out. The good man greeted me with a beaming face. "At last they are free and saved," he said, laughing with happiness. "Thanks to you. They are already on their way to the station. Your secretary went straight off with them. Oh, Your Highness, you are a kind and noble man!" He had tears in his eyes. He caught at my hand. He bent down to kiss it. The canaries trilled in their cage.

I wrenched my hand away from him, turned around without a word, jumped into the cab, and drove back to my hotel.

On the way, I took the cheque out of my pocket and clutched it convulsively. It was my blood money, but it should become my atonement. It was an unbelievably high reward. Even today I am ashamed to mention the sum— although I have told you all the other shameful details. No more Lutetia, no more dressmaker, no more Krapotkin. Back to Russia! With money I could still overtake them at the frontier. Telegraph my colleagues. They knew me. With money they could be sent back. No more ridiculous ambitions. I must make amends! Amends! Pack my bags and back to Russia. To save. To save those souls!

I paid my hotel bill. Ordered my bags to be packed. I called for drinks. I drank. I drank. A wild rejoicing filled me. I was already saved. I telegraphed to Kaniuk, the chief of our frontier police; told him to detain the Rifkins. I packed furiously, assisted by two valets.

Shortly before midnight I was ready. My train did not leave until seven o'clock in the morning. I put my hand in my pocket and felt a key. By its shape, by its wards, my fingers knew it for the key of Lutetia's house. Ah, it was the pointing finger of God. I would go to her tonight, this blessed night, and confess and tell her everything. I would say farewell and bestow freedom on myself and her.

I drove to Lutetia. Even as I stepped out into the fresh air I seemed to realize that I had drunk too much. All around I saw singing, excited people. I saw men with flags, excited speakers, sobbing women. At that time, as you know, Jaurès had been shot in Paris. Everything that I saw of course meant war. But I was so wrapped up in myself that I understood nothing; I—a mad and drunken fool. . . .

•   •   •

I had made up my mind to tell Lutetia that I had lied to her. Once on the road to so-called decency, nothing could hold me back. At that moment I intoxicated myself with decency, just as I had formerly intoxicated myself with evilness. Only much later did I realize that such a delirium cannot last. It is impossible to intoxicate oneself on decency. Virtue is always sober. Yes, I wanted to confess everything. I wanted—and it seemed to me infinitely tragic—to humble myself before my beloved, before taking leave of her for ever. That noble and pious renunciation seemed to me at that moment to be far finer than the fictitious aura of nobility in which I had been living, finer even than my passion. From now on I wanted to wander through the world, a suffering, nameless hero. If, so far in my life, I had been a pitiable hero, from now on I should be a real one.

In this mood of exalted depression—if I may call it that—I drove to Lutetia. It was just the hour at which she usually expected my visit. But even in the hall I was surprised to find that her maid did not come hurrying towards me, for she, too, was usually awaiting me. All the doors were open. In order to reach the pale blue bedroom which Lutetia called her "boudoir," I had to walk past the brightly-lit drawing room, with its hateful parrot and the rest of the menagerie, and then past her dressing room. At first I hesitated; I don't know why. Then I advanced with a lighter step than usual. The third door, that of the bedroom, was closed, but not locked. I opened it softly.

In the bed, beside Lutetia, with an arm around her neck, lay a man. And the man, as you may have guessed, was young Krapotkin. Both seemed to be so fast asleep that they had not heard me enter. I approached the bed on tiptoe. Oh, it was not my intention to make a so-called scene! At that moment the sight before my eyes caused me deep pain. But I was in no wise jealous. In the mood of heroic renunciation which then possessed me, the pain which the two caused me was almost desirable. In a way it confirmed my heroism and my decision. It was actually my intention to waken them gently, to wish them luck, and tell them everything. But at that moment Lutetia awoke and let out a shrill scream, which naturally roused the young man. Before I could say anything, he sat up in bed, in a pair of sky blue pyjamas which exposed his naked chest. It was a white, weakly, hairless boy's chest; a chest which, I know not why, aroused me to fury. "Ah, Golubchik," he said—and rubbed his eyes, "so we have not finished with you yet. Hasn't my secretary finally paid you? Give me my coat, you may take my wallet."

Lutetia was silent. She stared at me. She must already have known everything.

Since I made no movement, but only stood gazing sadly at the Prince, he, in his stupidity, may have thought that I was staring at him impertinently or threateningly. For he suddenly began to shout: "Get out! You spy, you scoundrel, you hireling—get out!"

And since I saw at that very moment how Lutetia sat up in bed, naked, with naked breasts, there awoke within me, in spite of all my resolutions and although I was already free from all fleshly desire, the old, evil rage. There flamed up in me, I say, at the sight of that naked woman who, according to the stupid conventions of men, should really have "belonged" to me, an uncontrollable madness.

At that moment I could think of nothing. Only one word—Golubchik—filled my brain and my blood; and my hate found no other expression. Lutetia's nakedness bewildered me, and louder even than the Prince had shouted, I yelled into his face: *"Your* name is Golubchik! Not mine! Who knows with how many Golubchiks your mother slept! No one knows. But mine slept with the old Krapotkin! And I am his son!"

He sprang up, he gripped me by the throat, the weakling. And he was even weaker because he was undressed. His delicate hands could not encircle my throat. I pushed him back. He fell on the bed.

From then on I no longer know what really happened. Even today I can still hear Lutetia's shrill screams. Even today I can still see how she sprang out of bed, completely naked, shameless it seemed to me then, to protect the youth. I was no longer conscious of my actions. In my pocket lay a heavy bunch of keys to which was attached an iron padlock, that lock which I used as a special precaution to secure my case when it contained particularly valuable papers. I had no valuable papers left. I was no longer a spy. I was a decent man. I was being tormented. I was being driven to murder. Without knowing what I did, I plunged my hand into my trouser pocket. Like a madman I struck out, at Krapotkin's head, at Lutetia's head. Until that hour I had never struck a blow in anger. I do not know how it affects other men when anger possesses them. But in my case, at all events, I know that every blow I struck filled me with an unfamiliar delight. At the same time I seemed to know that my blows gave an equal pleasure to my victims. I struck, I struck—I am not ashamed to describe it—I struck like that, my friends, and that—"

At these words Golubchik stood up from his chair, and his face at which we, his listeners, were staring, grew alternately ashen white and livid purple. He crashed his fist down on the table—again and again. The half-filled schnapps glasses fell over and rolled on to the floor. Our host hastened to save the carafe. Although he was feverishly watching Golubchik's movements, he nevertheless found the (professional) presence of mind to conceal the carafe in his lap. First Golubchik forced his eyes open, then he closed them; then his eyelids began to quiver, and a thin trickle of saliva worked into a white foam on his bluish lips. Yes, just so must he have looked when he committed the murder. In that moment we all knew for certain: he *was* a murderer. . . .

He sat down again. The color flowed back into his face. He dried his mouth with the back of his hand, and the hand on his handkerchief. Then he continued:

"At first I saw in Lutetia's forehead, above her left eye, a deep gash. The blood was spurting out and running down over her face and staining the pillows. Although Krapotkin, my second victim, lay close beside her, I succeeded in persuading myself that he was not there. (It was a wonderful gift not to see with open eyes what I did not want to see.) I only saw the torrent of Lutetia's blood. I was not horrified at my crime. No! I was only horrified at the ceaseless stream, at the superabundance of blood that could be contained in a human skull. It was as though I must soon— should I wait—be drowned in the blood which I myself had spilled.

I became suddenly quite calm. Nothing soothed me so much as the certainty that they would now both be silent. Silent for all eternity. Everything was quiet; only the cats came creeping in. They jumped on to the bed. Perhaps they smelled the blood. In the next room the parrot screeched my name, my stolen name: "Krapotkin! Krapotkin!"

I walked over to the mirror. I was quite calm. I watched my face and said to my reflection in a loud voice: "You are a murderer!" Immediately afterwards I thought: "You are in the police. A man must know his job thoroughly."

At that I walked into the lavatory, followed by the noiseless cats. I washed my hands and the keys and the padlock.

• • •

I sat down at Lutetia's unpleasantly ornate writing table and wrote a few words in a disguised handwriting. They were senseless words. They ran: "We always wished to die. And now we have died at the hands of another. Our murderer is a friend of my lover, the Prince."

It gave me a peculiar pleasure to copy Lutetia's handwriting. Indeed, it was not difficult, with her pen and her ink. She wrote like all petty-minded, middle-class women who have suddenly been raised above their accustomed *milieu*. Nevertheless I spent an unusually long time in copying her hand exactly. Round about me crept the cats. From time to time the parrot called: "Krapotkin! Krapotkin!"

After I had finished I left the room. I locked the

bedroom door on the outside, and also the outer door. I walked down the stairs calmly, without a thought in my head. As usual, I greeted the concièrge politely. In spite of the late hour she was still in her *loge* and when I passed she even stood up, for I was a prince—and she had often received princely tips from me.

I stood for a while in front of the house, calmly and patiently. I was waiting for a cab. When an empty one came along, I waved to it and climbed in. I drove to the Swiss shoemaker with whom the Rifkins had lived. I roused him out of bed and said: "You must hide me."

"Come," he said simply—and led me into a room which I had not seen before. "You will be safe here," he said. And he brought me milk and bread.

"I have something to tell you," I said. "I have not killed for political reasons, but for private ones."

"That does not concern me," he answered.

"I have something more to tell you," I said.

"What?" he asked.

At that moment—it was quite dark in the room—I summoned up the courage to say: "I am—I am a police spy. I have been one for many years. But today I committed a private murder."

"You can stay here until dawn," he said. "Until then—and not a second longer will you remain in this house." And then, as though an angel had awoken within him, he added: "Sleep well, and God forgive you!"

I did not sleep at all—need I tell you that? Long before

dawn I got up. I had lain there fully dressed, sleepless. I had to leave the house, and I left it. I wandered aimlessly through the awakening streets. When it struck eight o'clock from the various church towers, I tamed my steps towards the Embassy. I was not wrong in my reckoning. Without having been announced, I walked into Solovejczk's room. I told him everything.

After I had finished, he said:

"You have had much misfortune in your life, but also a little luck. You do not know what has happened. There is war in the world. It may break out at any moment. It may have already done so. Perhaps at the hour when you committed your misdeed, or let us rather say, your murder. You must return home. Wait half an hour. You shall go back."

• • •

"Well, my friends, I returned to Russia—gladly. In vain I inquired at the frontier for the Rifkins. Not even Kaniuk was to be found there. Nothing was known of my telegram. For all of you who have been through the war, there is no need to describe what it was—that World War. Death was near to everyone of us. We were as familiar with it as with a twin brother. Most of us feared it. But I—I sought it. I sought it with all my soul and all my strength. I sought it in the trenches, I sought it in outposts, between the barbed wire entanglements and in raiding parties, in poison gas and in every place where I might possibly have found it. I received decorations, but never a wound. It was simply that death shunned me. Death despised me. All around, my comrades fell in heaps. I mourned them not at all. I only mourned the fact that I could not die. I had murdered, and I could not die. I had brought a sacrifice to death, and death punished me: Me, me alone, it refused to have.

At that time I longed for it. For I believed then that death was an agony by which one could atone. Only later did I begin to realize that it was a deliverance. I had not earned it; and therefore it had not come to deliver me.

It is unnecessary to remind you, my friends, of all the disasters which overtook Russia. They have, indeed, nothing to do with my story. To my story belongs only the fact that, against my desire and will, I escaped the Revolution unharmed and fled to Austria. From there I went to Switzerland.

But there is no need to tell you the various stages of my flight. It eventually brought me to France; it brought me to Paris. After death had disdained me, I was drawn back to the scene of my miserable crimes, to the scene of my murder.

I arrived in Paris. It was a joyous day, although autumn was already merging into winter. But winter in Paris looks very like our Russian autumn. Everywhere people were celebrating victory and peace. But what had victory to do with me, what did I care for peace? I turned my steps towards the house in the Champs Élysées, where I had once committed a murder.

The concièrge, the old concièrge of former days, was still standing before the door. She did not recognize me. How could she have recognized me? I had grown gray— gray as I am today.

I inquired for Lutetia—and my heart thumped.

"Third floor left," she said.

I climbed the stairs. I rang the bell. Lutetia herself opened the door. I recognized her immediately. She did not recognize me. She seemed about to shut the door.

"Ah," she said after a while—stepped backwards, shut the door, and then opened it again. "Ah," she repeated, and held out her arms.

I do not know why I fell into those arms. We embraced long and passionately. I felt clearly that the situation was unbelievably banal, ridiculous, even grotesque. Just think. I was holding in my arms the woman whom I believed I had killed with my own hands.

Well, my friends, I experienced the greatest—the deepest, if you like—of all tragedies: the tragedy of banality.

I stayed with Lutetia. Actually, she had long since ceased to be called that—and the name of the fashionable dressmaker, too, had passed into oblivion. So I stayed with her. From love, from remorse, from weakness—who knows?

I had killed neither of them. The Rifkins were probably the only ones I had killed. The day before yesterday I met young Prince Krapotkin in the Jardin du Luxembourg. Accompanying him was his bearded, silver and black secretary, who still lived and who, although thinner and shabbier than formerly, still looked less like the companion of a prince than his pallbearer, his mourner. The young Prince was hobbling along on two sticks—perhaps as a result of the injuries which I had inflicted on his head.

"Ah, Golubchik," he called when he saw me—and his voice sounded different, almost happy.

"Yes, it is I," I said. "Forgive me."

"Nothing, nothing, nothing of the past," he said, and with the aid of his two sticks drew himself up to his full height. "Only the present, the future, is important."

I saw immediately that he was weak in his mind, and said: "Yes, yes."

Suddenly a feeble fire glowed in his eyes, and he asked: "Mademoiselle Lutetia? Is she still alive?"

"She is alive," I said and hastily took my leave.

·   ·   ·

"And that is really the end of my story," said Golubchik, the murderer. "I had a few more remarks to make. . . .

It was growing light. One could feel it even through the closed shutters. Through the chinks penetrated the victorious golden light of a summer's morning, faint and yet strong. Outside could be heard the awakening noises of the Paris streets and, above all, the loud chorus of the birds.

We were all silent. Our glasses had long stood empty.

Suddenly there came a hard, sharp knocking on the shutter outside the door. "That's her!" muttered Golubchik, our "murderer"—and in the next moment he had vanished. He had hidden himself under the table.

The host of the "Tari-Bari" walked leisurely across to the door. He opened it. He inserted—and to us it seemed to last an eternity—the great key into the lock; and slowly, slowly and reluctantly, the iron roller-shutter creaked upwards. The new day flowed in, full and triumphant, into our nocturnal yesterday. But more determined even than the morning light, an elderly, withered woman pushed her way into the restaurant. She looked more like an over-grown, emaciated bird than a woman. A short black veil, clumsily sewn to the left edge of her ridiculous hat, tried in vain to conceal a deep hideous scar over her left eye. And the shrill voice in which she asked: "Where is my Golubchik? Is he here? Where is he?" frightened us all so much that, had we even been willing, we would have been unable to tell her the truth. She cast a few vicious and inhumanly sharp glances around the room—and then left.

A few moments later Golubchik crept out from underneath the table.

"She has gone!" he said, relieved. "That was Lutetia." And immediately afterwards: "*Auf Wiedersehen*. My friends. Until tomorrow evening!"

With him also went the chauffeur. Outside the first customer was already waiting. He was hooting impatiently on his horn.

·　　·　　·

Our host remained alone with me. "What stories one hears in your restaurant!" I said.

"Quite ordinary, quite ordinary," he replied. "What is there strange in life? It gives us nothing but ordinary stories. But that won't stop you coming again, I hope?"

"Of course not!" I said.

When I spoke those words, I was convinced that I would often again see the restaurant and its owner and the murderer Golubchik and all the other guests. I went out.

Our host thought it necessary to accompany me to the threshold. It looked as though he were still slightly doubtful of my intention to continue visiting his restaurant. "You will really come again?" he asked once more. "But of course," I said. "You know that I live just across the road, in the Hotel des Fleurs Verts." "I know, I know," he said, "but it suddenly seemed to me as though you were already far away."

These unexpected words did not exactly frighten me, but I was greatly surprised by them. I felt that they contained some great and as yet unknown truth. Of course, it was nothing more than conventional politeness that made the host of the "Tari-Bari" walk with me to the door; for I was only a regular guest, who had shared in a somewhat alcoholic night. And yet there was something solemn, something unusually, I might almost say, unjustifiably, solemn about this procedure. The first carts were already returning from the markets. They rattled gaily along, although the drivers, wearied by their night's work, were asleep, and the reins in their sleeping hands seemed to be asleep too. A blackbird came hopping boldly up to the restaurant keeper's shabby, loose felt slippers. It stood calmly beside us, as though sunk in thought and yet interested in our conversation. The diverse sounds of morning were awakening to life. Doors opened gratingly, windows rattled softly, brooms swept harshly over the pavements, and somewhere a child was crying, having perhaps been startled from its sleep. "This is a morning like any other morning," I said to myself. "An ordinary Parisian summer morning." And aloud I said to our host: "But I'm not going away. I'm not thinking of it." And at that I gave a little irresolute laugh. It should have been a strong, convincing laugh, but unfortunately it emerged as such a miserable effort: a real abortion of a laugh. . . .

"Well then, *auf Wiedersehen*," he said, and I pressed his soft, fleshy hand.

I did not look around at him again. But I sensed that he had gone back into his restaurant. It was, of course, my intention to cross the street and return to my hotel. But I did not do so. It seemed to me that the morning lured me into taking a little stroll and I felt that it would be stupid, if not indeed wicked, to return to a stuffy room at a time when one could not say that it was either too early or too late. It was no longer early morning, and it was not yet late. I decided to walk around the block a few times.

I do not know how long I wandered round. When I finally stood in front of the door of my hotel, I could remember no more of my stroll than the uncounted tolling of bells from several unknown church clocks. The sun was already shining strongly into the hall. The owner of the hotel, in pink shirt sleeves, seemed as though he were already perspiring as he did only at noon on other days. At any rate, although he was doing nothing at the moment, he had an extremely occupied expression on his face. I immediately learned why.

"At last a visitor!" he exclaimed, and pointed at three trunks which he had piled up beside his desk. "Look at the luggage," he said, "and you can see straight away what sort of a visitor we've got!"

I looked at the pile. There were three yellow pigskin trunks, and their brass locks shone like tightly closed, golden mouths. Over each lock there stood, in blood-red lettering, the initials: "J.L."

"He has room twelve," said my hotel keeper. "Just next to yours. I always put fine visitors next door to one another."

With that he handed me my key.

I held the key for a while in my hand and then returned it to him. "I will drink my coffee down stairs," I said. "I am too tired to go up."

I drank my coffee in the little writing room, between a dried-up ink pot and a majolica vase filled with celluloid violets which reminded me of All Souls Day.

Suddenly the glass door opened and in stepped, no, tripped, an elegant gentleman. From him there emanated, curiously enough, a strong smell of violets, so that for the first moment I thought that the celluloid flowers in the majolica vase had come to life. At each step the man's left foot—I could see it plainly—described a neat little circle. He was dressed entirely in light gray; indeed he seemed enveloped in a silvery summer of his own. His hair shone blue-black. It was parted austerely down the middle and looked as though it had been smoothed not with a comb but with a tongue.

He nodded to me, amiably and at the same time reservedly.

"Another coffee!" he called through the door, which he had left open.

That "another" annoyed me.

For a long time, for an unnecessarily long time, he stirred the spoon around in his cup.

I was just about to get up when he began to speak, in a voice that sounded like flutes and velvet, like a velvet flute:

"You are a stranger here, are you not?"

It rang in my ears like an echo. I remembered that I had already heard that same question today—or was it yesterday? Yes. That question . . . the murderer Golubchik had mentioned it . . . he had spoken it last night; or perhaps it had not been worded quite like that. At the same time I recalled the name: "Jenö Lakatos," and I saw again the blood-red initials on the yellow trunks: "J.L."

So instead of answering the man, I asked:

"How long are you intending to stay here?"

"Oh, I have time enough," he answered. "My time is my own."

The hotelier came in with a blank registration form. He requested the new guest to fill in his name.

"Write," I said—although he had never asked me, I being overcome by an access of impertinence for which, even today, I cannot account—"write, under surname: 'Lakatos,' under Christian name: 'Jenö.'" And I got up and bowed and went out.

.   .   .

On the same day I left my quarters in the Rue des Quatres Vents. Golubchik I have never seen since, nor any of the men who sat that night listening to his story.